An Olde Concord Christmas

An Olde Concord Christmas

THE MUSEUM OF

THE CONCORD ANTIQUARIAN SOCIETY

CONCORD, MASSACHUSETTS

ST. MARTIN'S PRESS / NEW YORK

1980

ALSO BY THE MUSEUM

The Flavour of Concord

Mary R. Fenn, Museum history and tour

Elizabeth R. Mottur, holiday recipes

Louise M. Nelson, photograph captions

Elizabeth H. Wilson, holiday decorations

Wood engravings by Michael McCurdy

St. Martin's Press, Inc.

175 Fifth Avenue

New York, N.Y. 10010

Manufactured in the United States of America

The Museum can be reached by taking the Massachusetts Turnpike to Route 128 North to Route 2 West. Follow the sign to Concord Center off Route 2. The Museum is at the intersection of Route 2A and Cambridge Turnpike, one mile from Route 2. Information on rates, hours, and group reservations can be obtained by calling the Museum office at (617) 369-9609.

Library of Congress Cataloging in Publication Data

The Museum of the Concord Antiquarian Society

An olde Concord Christmas.

Based on the collections of the Concord Antiquarian Society Museum.

1. Christmas—Massachusetts—Concord—Exhibitions.
2. Christmas decorations—Massachusetts—Concord.
3. Christmas cookery. 4. Concord Antiquarian Society, Concord, Mass. Museum. I. Concord Antiquarian Society, Concord, Mass. Museum. II. Title.

GT4986.M37S77   394.2'68282'097444   80–14561

ISBN 0–312–58421–0

Contents

How to Make Your Own Olde Concord Christmas Decorations

Foreword

Imagine for a moment a room of lovely proportions with original eighteenth-century paneling painted a soft musty blue-green, a large gateleg table in the center surrounded by finely carved bannister-back side chairs, early engravings on the wall, a dressing table with a looking glass of the Queen Anne period hung over it, a fire crackling in the fireplace, the only other light from candles flickering in brass candlesticks. Imagine now a woman with a great love of history, antiques, and period flower arranging finding herself in this room on a winter's day with snow falling gently outside the small paned windows. The room is one of the period rooms at the Museum of the Concord Antiquarian Society. The woman is Betty Hale, and it was in 1969 that she suggested to the Board of the Concord Garden Club that its members decorate the Museum's rooms as they might have been for Christmases past.

This is how it all began, the Museum exhibit that has since attracted national attention, has been photographed by *Antiques, Yankee, Redbook, Gourmet,* and *House Beautiful's Home Decorating,* has been seen year after year by thousands of people, and has inspired this book.

The Museum is made up of a series of period rooms that span the first two hundred years of Concord's history. A tour begins in the simplest early dwelling and progresses through fourteen rooms, ending with a room of Empire splendor. The first year the Museum was dressed for Christmas, 1969, the exhibit was open to the public for only one day, but it was greeted with such enthusiasm by all who saw it, and it was so rewarding to those who did the research and appointed the rooms, that it has been done every other year since with a growing number of volunteers and guests. In 1978 over 4,400 attended, there were over 400 volunteers involved, and it was open for ten days. In recent years a large tent has been imported so that no one would have to wait in the cold. With the growth in size of the audience and the amount of publicity, numerous other museums and historic houses have discovered the pleasures of similar exhibits.

Of course there have been many changes and refinements during these ten years. Music, both live and taped, has been added to some of the settings; luncheon has been served at the neighboring First Parish Church; the Museum's own Flower Committee and other volunteers now do the research and decorations, stage an elaborate Preview Party, and serve coffee, cider, and homemade muffins. Some of the rooms have been refurbished to better reflect early Concord taste. Two rooms and the hallway have been repapered with reproductions of wallpapers found in Concord homes; another has been stenciled with patterns found locally. This year, 1980, with the completion of the Cummings Davis Building now under construction, an even more extensive exhibit is planned, which will include both concerts and lectures.

And the research continues. Though it is difficult to find a great deal of primary source material on Christmases in Concord in the seventeenth and eighteenth centuries, there is an enormous amount of historical data. By studying this and learning as much as possible about the living habits and social attitudes, the decorators have attempted to surmise what might have been. In all it takes a whole year to prepare for this exhibit, and, although there may have been some similarity to the themes, no room is ever done just as it was done before.

Dealing with the fact that the earliest settlers not only did not celebrate Christmas but also were strongly opposed to any form of revelry or gift-giving has presented the biggest challenge. Plainly and simply, the Puritans banned the celebration of Christmas. This being so, the earliest rooms are treated as if for a family gathering and a celebration of a successful harvest, and the deep religious convictions of the Puritans are emphasized by the ever-present Bible and Bible boxes. In 1681 the anti-Christmas ban was lifted, and the rigid regime of the Puritans became increasingly weakened with the tremendous increase in prosperity of the colonies. In *Paul Revere and the World He Lived In,* Esther Forbes makes reference to the Christmas greens and bayberry candles used to decorate Christ's Church in Boston in the 1740s. While "An Olde Concord Christmas" may cause a strict historian some uneasiness, it is hard to believe that the lady of the household in the 1600s would not have gathered some lovely red berries and brought them into her humble house for a touch of color on a bleak New England winter day. While this is admittedly an idealized and romanticized version of the past, in a world increasingly dominated by computer technology and numbered plastic cards, it is refreshing to remove oneself to an earlier time, a time when bigger and brighter did not necessarily mean better. The soft candlelight, the smells of fresh greens and hot cider, the sound of the harpsichord, the sight of a few red partridgeberries and soft velvet ribbons, all combine to create a lovely atmosphere in which to begin the Christmas season.

It is very exciting to present this book as an example of Concord, its people, and its past as seen through its Museum. Concord is a very special place, a place of high thinking, a community of robust talent and intellect. It is a town with a great history that brings out the best in the people who live in it, who govern it, and who preserve and interpret its past in the process of creating its future. These are the people who bring its history to life in this Museum, who continue to give tirelessly of their time and skills. This book is a tribute to them, to all who have worked so hard to present this exhibit over the past ten years. It is hoped that it will be helpful to others who are attempting the same sort of thing either in their own homes or in museums and historic houses. We owe a special vote of thanks to the hardy band that celebrated this past Christmas by preparing this manuscript—Mary Fenn, Louise Nelson, Libby Wilson, and Libby Mottur, and especially to Weezie Johnson, who put all the parts together and made them sing.

Caroline Stride, Director
January 1980

THE MUSEUM

The Story of the Museum of the Concord Antiquarian Society

The story of the Museum of the Concord Antiquarian Society begins with a strange little man named Cummings E. Davis, who lived in Concord in the nineteenth century. One time he took a notion to collect old trash: things that people were throwing out or selling for a pittance just to get rid of them. Everyone shook his head sadly and said that Davis had become definitely queer. Who would want old colonial cradles or farm tools or handmade chairs when one could buy the stylish ornate Victorian things then in vogue? Davis even got hold of a dilapidated chest he found in someone's barn being used for feed for the cows. Well, it did have a pretty design carved on the front. Who would ever dream that that chest would become the nucleus of one of the finest collections of furniture in the country? Davis had no inkling that his collection would ever become valuable, but he did have an idea that it might make some money for him. He rented an upstairs room in the courthouse and charged a fee for visitors to view it. He counted on the many tourists who came to Concord to visit our first inland community, the place that saw the beginning of the Revolutionary War, and the houses of the famous authors. To further advertise his little collection, Davis dressed in a Revolutionary-style costume: knee breeches, an old coat, and a tricorne hat. The townspeople shook their heads even more and said, "How sad."

But there are always a few people in any community who look ahead and appreciate the value of what others do not see. It occurred to some of the townsmen that Davis's collection might be valuable. There wasn't even a historical society in Concord, but they decided to do something about it; in 1886, they founded the Concord Antiquarian Society, bought Davis's collection, and hired him to continue as curator. Realizing that many tourists missed seeing the collection because they were too weary from sightseeing to climb the stairs in the courthouse, they looked about for a better location, and bought the Reuben Brown house on Concord's main road. Installing Davis and his collection in the house, they made some attempt to display the artifacts according to periods. It was fortunate indeed that the house happened to be for sale at that time, for it was large and roomy, and geographically just right. What's more, it was one of the oldest houses in Concord, having been built in 1667.

As time went on, the collection became crowded, and since extensive repairs were needed in the building, the Concord Antiquarian Society decided to erect a new, spacious building, as nearly fireproof as possible, and make it of brick in the colonial style. They proposed to have each room represent a certain period so that visitors, then as now, might walk through the Museum and see the changes in style following the growth and development of the country. Through the generosity of Ralph Waldo Emerson's family, the "heater piece" adjoining his house next door was acquired. This V-shaped lot between Lexington Road and the Cambridge Turnpike got its name because it was in the shape of a flatiron.

Money was raised for the project, many of the old families giving substantial sums. Harry B. Little, the architect, donated his services, and Russell H. Kettell, the first director, gave a great deal of fine old paneling for the interiors. The building was completed and the furnishings moved in 1930. A seventeenth-century house, which was about to be torn down, was moved to Concord from Ipswich and added at an angle to the long ell. This allowed room for a semi-enclosed outdoor garden where old fashioned herbs, lilacs, and an espaliered pear tree were planted. Two straw bee skeps were placed against the wall of the house.

Decorating the Museum for An Olde Concord Christmas takes an entire year, largely because of the extensive research needed to make sure that each room's decor is authentic for its period. For that reason, the exhibition is given only every other year, much to the disappointment of many people who begin calling in the spring to learn when the exhibition will take place, and to make reservations. When we think of Christmas decorations, the first thing that comes to mind is a Christmas tree, but Christmas trees were unknown in New England until Victorian times, and that period is represented by only one room in the Museum. To be sure, the early settlers came from England, where Christmas was celebrated with decorations, song, and revelry. Although they brought many of their old customs with them to the new country, they looked upon any celebration of Christmas (except going to church) as blasphemous. Furthermore, they wished no trace of the despotic Church of England, from which they had fled, to interfere with their solemn convictions. Plus, the Pilgrims' long sojourn in Holland resulted in a whole generation of children who knew nothing of the English Christmas tradition.

It was the Pilgrims' devout religious conviction that since all things came from God, any disaster was a sign that the people had displeased God. In such cases as floods or droughts, the minister and selectman would call for a Fast Day in which every form of pleasure, even eating, was denied. Now just suppose a celebration such as Christmas should be scheduled on a specified date that coincided with a time of God's displeasure. One shudders to think of the consequences.

Even though only natural materials gathered from the woods are used in decorating the Museum, more research is needed to be certain that a particular berry, for example, had been introduced into the country at the time of the period to be represented. Greens on the endangered list must also be avoided. Colors to be used must be coordinated with the colors of the furniture and wallpaper, and the scale of each decoration must be carefully worked out. Programs are printed. Each of fourteen rooms and halls must have one guide assigned for the morning hours and another for the afternoon. This is in addition to scheduling ticket-takers, waitresses for the small snack bar, and the women in charge of all the rooms who check the candles to make sure they have not tipped, and who replace those that have burned nearly to the bottom. Police are hired to control the traffic, for, in the course of the ten-day exhibit, literally thousands of people come from all over New England, some groups arriving in chartered buses. The evening preview calls for more room guides, all of whom (with the daytime guides) have been briefed on the contents of the room to which they are assigned. Special costumes are provided for the guides and waitresses for the evening preview, and of course the refreshments must be prepared. One important item is working out a route for the visitors to follow through the rooms to avoid bottlenecks. Since the exhibition lasts for ten days, the food shown must be of a type that does not spoil. This is also true of the flowers, which are dried in such a skillful way that it is sometimes difficult to keep visitors from touching them to make sure they are not fresh. Members of the Ladies' Association take lessons in flower-drying technique.

1.

2. Decoration by Mrs. Richard E. Hale.

1. Candles light the windows and a pine wreath adorns the museum as seen at twilight.
2. Beyond the piled-up snow in the garden sits a seventeenth-century house. Here we will start a tour of the period rooms of the Museum of the Concord Antiquarian Society and see the rooms as they might have looked during the Christmas season in years past.

A Guided Tour of the Museum

THE COLONIAL PERIOD

The early settlers had come to Concord after a long voyage in a small sailing ship where space was at a premium. Only bare necessities could be brought, such as cooking vessels, chests to hold their belongings, the family Bible in its Bible box, a table to eat from, a chair for father with stools for the rest of the family, and a bed for the parents (the children slept on pallets on the floor). We read how their first habitations were Indian-style—half cave and half timbers—dug into the sandy ridge along the only road. In view of this, it is a wonder that anything has remained.

Gradually, as time went by, houses were built: rather large ones for the ministers, and smaller ones with leaded windows and often an overhanging second storey for ordinary people. The tour of the Museum begins with this late-seventeenth-century period (see photo #3, page 35). The huge fireplace dominated the downstairs room, for it afforded heat, cooking facilities, and even light during the dark New England winter days. Candles were expensive and tedious to make, so betty lamps and rushlights were used to augment the light from the fireplace. Occasionally a family might have a small Turkey carpet. This was too precious to walk on, so it was placed on the table. Although at this time living conditions had become a little easier, still everything in the house was strictly utilitarian. The oven tucked into the side of the great fireplace was for baking bread, pies, and pots of beans; the dried herbs hanging from the rafters were used for flavoring and medicines; the high-backed settle placed sideways to the fire kept out drafts; and the heavy studded door was for protection against wild animals and Indians. The only bit of decoration might be a bowl of bright red berries or a spray of bittersweet on a chest.

The next room represents the end of the seventeenth century, when people were able to furnish their homes more in accordance with the homes they had left in England. We often hear how the earliest houses in New England were log cabins. It would seem that this would have been the simplest and quickest way of construction. But these were Englishmen who came to our shores, and they built their houses of clapboards, as Englishmen did in the home country. It didn't matter that the boards had to be sawed by hand, a long tiring process; clapboards it was. Of course the meetinghouse, mills, and ministers' houses were built first, but by the end of the century substantial houses, many of which are still standing, were springing up along the Bay Road.

So we find in the Seventeenth-Century Room in the Museum the large fireplace again, the high-backed settle, and even a long wooden crane on which one might hang clothes to dry or throw a blanket over to keep in the heat about the fireplace area (see photo #6, page 36). We begin to find the furniture more decorative, for example, an old oak press (not pictured) with drawers, doors, and carving, which was one of the pieces originally owned by a Lexington man and acquired by Cummings Davis. On the wall is a framed piece of stump-work embroidery (not pictured) depicting the biblical story of Esther. It was made by nineteen-year-old Rebecca Wheeler in 1664 and is thought to be the earliest piece of this type of embroidery in America. Now we find the Bible box with a slanting top that could serve as a desk, a gateleg table, carved chairs, pewter, decorated wares from Delft, and even an early mirror, which was rare indeed, for mirrors had to be imported; all indicate a more gentle way of life (photo #4, page 35). A carved chest against the wall is the very one Cummings Davis rescued from a barn to start his collection (photo #5, page 35). Little did he know that it would be viewed and admired by visitors from all over the world. Since metal was almost nonexistent in the colonies, except for a small amount turned out by the Saugus Iron Works and another in Quincy, wood was used. Instead of iron spikes to hold beams together, wooden pegs were used. These were called *tree nails*, a term that came to be corrupted into *trunnels*. We find them today in many old Concord houses.

An object of great interest to visitors is a small cask with a strap, called a *rundlet*, which was used to carry rum (see windowsill, photo #5, page 35). As to why there was a strap, it was because the rundlet was taken to the fields to refresh the hard-working farmers from time to time, and the strap was hung around the neck, leaving the hands free. Rum was used a great deal in the early days. Even the minister laid in his winter's supply as a matter of course. There may have been excesses, but for the most part rum did not seem to affect the farmers. It is thought that their physical toil counterbalanced any ill effects. In a later period *switchel,* a drink made of molasses, vinegar, and herbs, was popular. This was also carried in a jug out to the fields to assuage the thirst of the farm workers. In the nineteenth century drinking became a social gesture, and sherry or other wines were served in the homes of the more affluent. Mrs. Alcott made beer from hops—the original hop vines still grow in her garden. She added various herbs for flavoring, and her husband, ever the naive, exclaimed that it was remarkable how that drink refreshed one when toiling in the vegetable garden. There is even a receipt showing that one of the deacons in the church took the steam cars to Boston and bought two gallons of Madeira wine for the communion. It does not tell us how often he had to make the trip.

A surprising item (not pictured) in this room is a far cry from the rundlet and all the stories of the use of spirits. It is a wooden box covered in velvet, lined with rose-colored silk, and studded with silver, which is said to have belonged to Queen Elizabeth I at the time when she was a princess and confined in prison by Mary Tudor. According to tradition, the box was given to Elizabeth's maid-in-waiting, coming down in her family.

Since no real Christmas decorations would have been seen in a room of this period, the exhibition has envisioned a family reunion. After the harvest was gathered and stored, the winter's supply of wood cut, and all the fall chores done, this was a welcome respite when relatives might get together for a family feast. On the table a bowl of assorted apples is placed, together with a sugar cone and the instrument for snipping off bits of sugar (photo #4, page 35). Fall vegetables and fruits are piled on one side of the hearth (photo #7, page 36), while nearer the fire are chestnuts, a round loaf of bread, and a dish of squash. A turkey is on the spit. The pewter tankards were shined, and the best pewter plates brought out to replace the wooden trenchers. Pomander balls made of apples, oranges, or lemons, were set about to dispel bad odors (photo #54, page 93).

Since iron was so scarce, the lug pole in the fireplace from which the cooking kettles hung was made of green wood. Naturally in time it would dry out and char, and finally break, dropping the kettle of food into the embers; and the family would lose its dinner. This is where we get the expression, "the fat is in the fire." An iron frying pan, called a *spider* (photo #7, page 36) because of its long handle and legs, could be pushed nearer or farther from the flames, or even set on top of the embers. From the rafters hang wild birds, which were shot in

Concord river meadows, and smoked codfish from Boston. An animal skin is thrown over the settle. It would have been used as protection against cold drafts (photo #6, page 36).

Leaving the Seventeenth-Century Room, we go through a passage where old signs are hung on the pine-sheathed walls. Although the first settlers had been educated in England, the second generation did not have schooling, and many could neither read nor write. However, a shop sign that showed a clock or a razor or a horse was quite understandable. To embellish the corridor for the exhibition, the Museum encircles a clock-shaped sign with laurel. It was this sign that served as the logo of the first exhibit, called "A Time of Christmas" (photo #10, page 37).

In this country, only a handful of rooms have survived that have floors, walls, and ceilings in pine. Such a room was found in Hampton, New Hampshire, and moved to the Museum in its entirety (with the exception of the windows, which have been reproduced (photos #11 and 12, page 38). The room is adjacent to the corridor of signs, and the doors of the room have leather hinges. No paint was used in the room originally, although some was added at a later date. The furnishings in this room were made in the first half of the eighteenth century. We find the chests now decorated with applied molding and line drawings. One, a forerunner of the tall chests to come, has a single drawer (photo #11, page 38).

An interesting feature of the Pine-Ceiled Room is a sanded floor; not a sand-scrubbed floor, but a floor that actually has sand on it. This was very practical. The sand would catch all the drips and spills, and when it got dirty, it could be swept out the door and replaced with new sand. Of course, if company were expected, the housewife might sweep the sand in whorls or other designs. It made no difference that the pattern was soon obliterated with footprints, as long as it looked well to greet the guests (photo #12, page 38).

Because there are no indications of Christmas in the room (as Christmas was not celebrated at this time), it has been arranged to represent a typical farmer's home. Eggs and vegetables are on the sideboard. Brightly polished apples and a few eating utensils can be seen on the table, although at this time one generally ate with a knife. To add a touch of beauty, the farmer's wife has placed some air-dried wildflowers in a crock.

The next room, known as the Crane Room, represents the early 1700s. Now we find that the fireplace has a metal lug pole from which hangs a tip kettle, a great convenience (photo #13, page 38). The lug pole is a crane that can be moved out to hang kettles on, then pushed back over the fire. The fireplace itself is more shallow, to throw the heat out into the room. On the hearth to the right of the fireplace is an iron bar with a knob on one end, called a *loggerhead* (photo #13, page 38). The knob rested in the glowing embers and could be thrust into a pewter mug of flip (a sweetened spice liquor to which beaten eggs were added) to heat it. It also happened that sometimes two old cronies sitting before the fire would get into an argument. When words failed, they would seize a loggerhead and wield it threateningly to emphasize a point. From this came the expression "at loggerheads." All sorts of metal utensils were in use at this time, such as trivets and even a toaster that held two slices of bread side by side. When the bread was toasted on one side, the toaster could be flipped around to let the other side face the fire. Sometimes a pot with embers in it held a pan where food was placed. On top was another container for embers, so that the food could be heated from both sides. From this we get the expression "between two fires."

The Crane Room is sometimes arranged as a barroom for the Christmas exhibit. Strong herbs to dispel unpleasant odors are hung from the fireplace. Rum is placed in large bowls, and whiskey is displayed in heavy bottles with accompanying stemmed glasses. Beer is set out in pewter mugs. At other times the Crane Room is arranged as a millinery shop with various styles of hats on display including a calash or folding bonnet, a tall silk hat, and even a mourning bonnet. On one occasion it was a penny shop, with wares arranged in the bay window (photo #14, page 39) and ribbons and yardgoods placed on the shelves. At another Christmas exhibit a large garland made of arborvitae, ferns, milkweed pods, and wheat was hung over the fireplace (photo #13, page 38).

As we pass from the Crane Room to the Relic Room we see a lighted cabinet tucked into a recess (photo #15, page 39). In it is the original Paul Revere lantern, which hung in the belfry of the Old North Church in Boston as a signal: "one if by land and two if by sea," as the familiar line from Longfellow's poem goes. Seven years after that fateful night when the British marched on Lexington and Concord, Captain Daniel Brown learned that one of the lanterns was still in the belfry, although the other had become lost. The sexton was willing to sell the lantern to Brown, and assured him of its authenticity. It was passed down from Brown to his son and then sold to Cummings Davis, and that is how one of America's most precious relics came to the Concord Museum. James Barrett's sword is hanging in the case as well, for Barrett had charge of all the supplies in Concord before the Revolution and of course was present at the fight at the bridge. A musket and powder horn are also displayed, as well as a British sword taken by one of the minutemen at the skirmish.

The Relic Room contains another of our country's treasures, a large oil painting done by Ralph Earle shortly after the battle of Lexington and Concord, (photo #16, page 39). It is one of four such scenes, two of the fight in Lexington and two in Concord. Some time later, Doolittle made some lithographs of the paintings that are so rare at the present time as to be museum pieces. Only the one original oil painting is known to be in existence. It shows two British officers standing on the hill burying ground watching the British troops marching into Concord. If the painter got carried away with the number of soldiers marching along, it was no more than appeared to the minutemen and militia assembled near the bridge on that day. The painting hung for many years in the home of Mrs. Stedman Buttrick, the very house where Colonel Jonathan Buttrick lived at the time of the Revolution, and where he mustered his men on the back lawn. Mrs. Buttrick once took her painting to the Museum of Fine Arts in Boston to be cleaned. When she went for it, the curator, who had had time to realize its significance, said, "Mrs. Buttrick, you have no right to keep this picture. It belongs to America." Mrs. Buttrick, a true Concordian with a mind of her own, remarked, "So I took my picture home." She did appreciate its importance, however, and said that her servants had strict orders that if the house ever caught on fire, they were to save first her two little dogs, Mutt and Jeff, and then the picture. She left it to the Museum in her will. As one would expect, Concord has grown considerably since 1775, but the views down Main Street and across Lexington Road have some familiar landmarks. Wright's Tavern in the foreground is still standing not far from the old meetinghouse, and some of the houses shown in the painting are familiar sights in town today. Concordians are, after all, well known for cherishing their old houses and their old clothes.

THE REVOLUTIONARY PERIOD

The early-eighteenth-century Green Room (photos #17–20, pages 40–41) is furnished as a dining room. The entire fireplace wall is paneled and painted a soft green. An awkward-looking homemade wing chair stands by the fireplace. It belonged to Dr. Philip Reed, who practiced in Concord in the second half of the seventeenth century. The side panels of the armchair were obviously added as an afterthought. Dr. Reed was a very outspoken man at a time when it did not pay to be outspoken. One time he publicly announced that a woman patient of his was made worse by having to stand for an hour in the meetinghouse during a pastoral prayer. Such a terrible offense did not go unnoticed, and since in the early days the town and the church were one, he was hauled before the court and fined twenty pounds.

Fine Chinese imports were highly prized during the early eighteenth century. The Museum owns a 125-piece set of handsome china dating from about 1822 (photos #18 and 19, pages 40–41). Its design is of butterflies, fruits, flowers, and birds in orange and gilt on white porcelain; it is believed that there is only one comparable set in the country, and that is privately owned. On the fireplace wall, behind the cupboard doors, which are closed for the exhibition, is a set of Imari china with a stunning design of peonies and crabs in red, blue, and gold.

On one wall of this room is a rare clock (not pictured), which dates from 1746. It was made by a well-known clock maker of that time named Mulliken, and has only one hand to show the time. A minute hand was not essential to a farm family. A long pendulum gives the clock the highly descriptive name of "wag on the wall." The handmade crewel curtains at the windows (not pictured) were made by the ladies of the Antiquarian Society and copied from an authentic design. In the mid-1700s they would have been used as bed curtains.

Since elaborate Christmas decorations were not known at this time, the Green Room has been prepared as though the family expects visitors from Boston. Because they would have come by sleigh, mugs of hot mulled cider await their arrival (photo #20, page 41), and chowder is being prepared in the adjoining kitchen. For the holiday season, a handsome cone of greens and lemons, with a pineapple for hospitality on top, is placed in the center of the table (photo #17, page 40). There is a mouth-watering roast turkey on the table, as well as round loaves of bread, mince pie, and dishes of sweets. On the side table is a handsome bouquet of yarrow, fake saffron, arborvitae, and pine, which complements the crewel curtains and the soft green of the paneling.

In our visit from room to room in the Museum we must keep in mind that in our own homes we have furnishings that have been handed down in the family as well as things that we have bought. So it is with the Museum. We find transition pieces, but for convenience, we name the rooms for the prevailing period. So it is with the Queen Anne Room, which represents the second half of the eighteenth century. Although certain artisans were congregating in centers like Philadelphia at this time, Concord was a country town, and local cabinetmakers were producing furniture in the current style. This was a time of elegance, at least among the more affluent families in the town. The side chairs in the room (photo #21, page 42) have the rounded tops and wide slats we associate with the Queen Anne style. To the left of the fireplace (photo #21, page 42) is a low slipper chair which was useful to tightly corseted ladies who found it difficult to bend low to put on their shoes. With England's acquisition of India, tea drinking came into vogue, so a tea table is ready for visitors (photo #22, page 42). The tea table and chair belonged to Abel Prescott, father of Dr. Samuel Prescott, who was coming home late one night from visiting his girl in Lexington when he overtook Paul Revere on his way to warn Concord that the British were coming. When Revere was stopped by an ambush of British soldiers, it was Prescott who leaped his horse over a stone wall and so was the one to warn the town.

A graceful dressing table between the windows (photo #24, page 43) was once owned by Thomas Dudley, governor of the Commonwealth. When Dudley was lieutenant governor, he married Governor Winthrop's daughter, and since the men considered themselves to be related by this tie, they called themselves brothers. Each of the men was granted a thousand acres of land along the Concord River; Winthrop's land lay to the south and Dudley's to the north. Two large boulders, known to this day as the Brother Rocks, mark the beginning of their land. A mirror made of one large piece of glass hangs on the wall above the dressing table. Until this time each mirror had two glasses, since there were no molds large enough for one. A small triangular spinet (photo #21, page 42) was manufactured in London by a famous spinet maker, Thomas Hitchcock, and shipped here without legs, which were added later. A tall clock (photo #21, page 42) has a brass plate with the name Nath'l Mulliken and the date 1746. Mulliken, whom we have met before, was one of America's first clock makers and lived in Lexington. Sliding wooden shutters in the windows (photo #21, page 42) were a protection against hostile Indians, or at least were useful in keeping out the cold. There are at least two privately owned houses in Concord that have these shutters.

The dark paneling on the fireplace wall of the Queen Anne Room makes a fine background for a large swag of field flowers, ferns, herbs, pansies, and hydrangea with apple green ribbons (photo #21, page 42). Variations of this design are made for different exhibitions; for example, one was made of boxwood and artemisia, decorated with lemons, yellow day lilies, feverfew, yarrow, daisies, and canterbury bells with soft yellow velvet ribbons (photo #25, page 43). A holiday party is the theme here, with molasses cake, mince tarts, and jumbals set out on the tea table. On a side table is a large bowl of negus, a drink containing port, water, sugar, lemon, and nutmeg (photo #58, page 94). It is wreathed in herbs. A small dish of candy and crystallized rose petals flanks the punch bowl. At one time the room was arranged for a puppet show with marionettes and all the accoutrements of the barker (photo #21, page 42).

The Chippendale Room dates from about 1760 to 1780 and also represents the period of prosperity that came to the colonies prior to the Revolution. Many advertisements appeared in the papers for wallpaper, Dutch tiles for "chiminies," and "East India chimey wares." It became the vogue to use the same color for curtains and furniture coverings. Thomas Chippendale was the foremost furniture designer at this time, and the designs in the room follow his styles. So we find chairs with the familiar perforated backs, and ball-and-claw feet (photo #26, page 44). The wing chair to the left of the fireplace belonged to Abel Moore, who lived on Lexington Road, next door to the Louisa May Alcott house. His son John reclaimed the wet meadows along the millbrook opposite his house by sanding the soil to make it productive. Since Moore was the town sheriff, he used the prisoners in the local jail as laborers. They were glad to have some outdoor work and also to receive a small fee. The Dutch tiles around the fireplace are of the soft lavender color called puce, which was very popular. The Pembroke table and a mirror (photo #28, page 45) once belonged to the Thoreau family. A handsome daybed and carved chair (not pictured) were the property of Peter Bulkeley, grandson of the Reverend Peter Bulkeley, who founded Concord in 1635.

The decorations for the Chippendale Room for An Olde Concord Christmas take their theme from the puce coloring in the tiles, curtains, and furniture coverings. The graceful decoration above the fireplace (photo #26, page 44) is formal in style, but is made colorful with velveteen and satin ribbons. It is apparent at a glance that visitors are expected, for a punch bowl rests on a silver tray, with cheese and crackers on a side dish (photo #27, page 45). On another table is a decanter with delicate wineglasses, a plate of tempting cookies, and a bowl of luscious fruits bought at the greengrocer's in Boston (photos #28 and 29, page 45). On a side table is displayed a beautiful topiary tree of boxwood and ribbons (photo #60, page 95).

Across the hall from the Chippendale Room is the Revolutionary Bedroom, so called because it dates from around 1775. The fireplace here (photo #34, page 46) is in the Chippendale style, but its being a bit more ornate indicates that it is of a later date. An impressive four-poster bed with its hangings dominates the room (photo #31, page 46). At the foot of the bed is a maple tea table (photo #33, page 46) that belonged to Dr. John Cuming, a public-spirited citizen and moderator at ninety town meetings from 1763 to 1788. Cuming went to the French and Indian Wars as a volunteer and was wounded, carrying a bullet in his hip for the rest of his life. He was appointed general in charge of the army that was to reinforce Gates in the Champlain valley, but remained at home at the urgent request of his wife. He continued to be active in the war effort, however, serving as a member of the Committee of Correspondence, a justice of the court, and a member of the House of Representatives and of the Constitutional Convention in 1799. Cuming never charged for a house call on the Sabbath. One can't help wondering how many of his patients found they could live with their affliction on Saturday, but found it necessary to call the good doctor on Sunday. At his death he left a sum of money to Harvard College, which was used to found the Harvard Medical School. The present Medical Center at the hospital in Concord is named in his honor. Along the wall of the room is a large chest on chest (photo #33, page 46) which has the date 1790 carved on the back.

A cherry slant-topped desk (photo #32, page 46) is thought to be the work of Joseph Hosmer, Concord's well-known cabinetmaker. Hosmer lived at the bend of the Sudbury River and, although he was a bachelor, built a fine home in 1757, next to his father's house. The new house was large enough to house his apprentices, and a small ell was his shop. Later he married Miss Lucy Barnes, and here they raised their family. Joseph Hosmer was very active in the affairs of the town, and at the time of the Revolution, joined the minutemen at the bridge. The particularly handsome wallpaper, a copy of a French Toile de Jouy print, is in a vivid blue.

The decorations in the Revolutionary Bedroom consist of pots of Jerusalem cherries flanking the fireplace, with greens, combined with ribbons and bittersweet, hanging on either side of the mantel (photo #34, page 46). At one exhibition the room represented Christmas morning, with a little girl in her ruffled nightgown and nightcap with streamers tied under her chin, just climbing out of the great bed. Although there would be no Christmas gifts at this time, she would look forward to this day as very special, for the family would attend a Christmas church service. Another time the room was prepared for a guest, with the covers turned down and a warming pan tucked under the bedclothes to make everything warm and cozy (photo #31, page 46). A thoughtful gesture was a decanter of sherry and a fruitcake on a side table. At the most recent Olde Concord Christmas, a Revolutionary soldier has come home from the war for a brief respite and to spend Christmas day with his family (photo #32, page 46). He sits at a desk, attending to his correspondence, with quill pen and sander. His shoes have been kicked off, and his feet in their handknit woolen stockings rest on a footstove. The suit he wears is the original minuteman costume that Daniel Chester French dressed his model in when he created the world-famous statue of a minuteman at the bridge.

Passing through the large hallway and up the stairs, one notices that the posts on the staircase (not pictured) were carved in groups of three, which was a common feature at the time. Five of the posts came from the actual staircase in John Hancock's house on Beacon Hill, which was demolished when the top of the hill was lowered. A very old watercolor (not pictured) on the stairs shows a view of a primitive Boston Common with the Hancock house in the background. The handsome wallpaper in the hallway, copied from that in an old house in Acton, has a large design of garlands; gray on gray (not pictured). Picking up this theme, laurel roping festoons the stair railing. On the sideboard in the hall below, a pyramid of frosted fruit flanked by candles gives a pleasing note of soft color (photo #61, page 95). A beautiful bouquet of dried flowers on the window ledge of the landing is so skillfully done that it is almost impossible to realize that they have not just been picked (photo #37, page 47).

THE FEDERAL PERIOD

As we go through the rooms on the second floor, the Federal style becomes apparent. All things change, and the overembellished European style of furniture caused a reaction to set in. Robert Adam and his brother, who were furniture designers, took a trip to Italy and became enamored of the classical revival there. Upon returning to England, Adam completely revolutionized English taste in furniture and houses. The new style was simple and delicate. Flutings, reedings, swags, Greek key designs, and pastel colors became all the rage. Soon books showing the new furniture by Adam, Hepplewhite, and Sheraton reached America, and their furniture was copied indiscriminately, making it difficult to distinguish between one artisan's style and another's. We notice that fireplaces, particularly in bedrooms, become smaller, and in what is called the Yellow Room, there is a cast-iron frame, similar to a Franklin stove. Although earlier woodwork and wallpaper colors were chosen for their durability, now lighter shades and more delicate styles predominate. Side chairs were often painted, and with the blossoming pride in the new country, patriotic designs were popular. The so-called Liverpool pitchers, made in Liverpool for the American sailors' trade, had pictures of Washington or fifteen stars representing the fifteen states of the Union or Masonic designs. Stenciling was popular, so the walls of the Yellow Room have recently been decorated along the ceiling, window, and door moldings, with stencils taken from an old design (stenciling not pictured). For the Christmas exhibit, the room is decorated as a child's room (photos #38 and 40, page 48). Dolls are placed on the bed, and a small table with a tiny tea set is at its foot. A kissing ball hangs from yellow ribbons in the window (photos #40 and 62, pages 48 and 95). Over the mantel is a green wreath with a large red bow. Decorating the wreath are small wooden toys (photo #39, page 48).

A charming bedroom, known as the Reeded Room because of the fine wood-work of that style, represents the period of about 1800. The bureau, chairs, and desk are all the work of Joseph Hosmer (photo #44, page 49). Two of the chairs were made for James Barrett, captain of the minutemen. A corner cupboard has the name Judah Potter and the date 1725 painted on the front in large letters (photo #42, page 49). Potter's house, said to have been built in 1723, unfortunately was destroyed by fire in 1731; Potter himself died in the fire. One wonders how the cupboard survived. Several pieces of funereal embroidery hang on the wall, for they were greatly in vogue at this time when nothing was so much enjoyed as death and the sadness that went with it. Probably because the people who lived here were so accustomed to the mournful pictures, they did not detract from the happy holiday spirit. On one occasion two rooms represented a Christmas wedding. The Reeded Room showed the charming confusion of the brides-maids' preparations. Gloves lay on the bedspread, and small bouquets with their bright ribbons. Boxes of wedding presents were placed on chairs and table tops. A tea table was set up at the foot of the bed, with decanter, stemmed wine-glasses, and a plate of fruitcake. Just to make it more realistic, one of the wine-glasses was half empty.

The Federal Parlor is sometimes called the McIntire Room. Samuel McIntire, a wood-carver and architect in Salem, greatly influenced architecture in New England in the early 1800s. He in turn was influenced by Adam, but added his own innovations to the classical style. For example, he made use of the American eagle, which was so popular at this time. The furniture in the Federal Parlor dates from about the beginning of the nineteenth century. The tall wall clock was about 1809, the sofa 1811, and the piano 1790 (photo #48, page 50). Engravings of patriotic subjects were popular both in England and America, and two such engravings of the Battle of Bunker Hill hang on the wall (not pictured). They were printed in England in 1789. A pair of side dishes made of Waterford glass may be seen in this room; they belonged to the Thoreau family (photo #46, page 50). It is amusing to see the amazement on visitors' faces when these pieces are pointed out, for they think of Henry Thoreau as living in a rough hut at Walden Pond for all of his life. Actually Thoreau lived in his well-built clapboard and plaster house for only two years, which was no more remarkable than many a young person today who tries his wings away from the family home and takes an apartment in Boston. To be sure, Thoreau's hut at Walden Pond did not include Waterford glass, for he was the prime advocate of the simple life. But his family lived in one of the larger houses in Concord, and it was beautifully furnished.

For the exhibition, the Federal Parlor was once decorated to represent a wedding reception, even to having a bride and bridesmaid dressed in authentic finery (photo #48, page 50). Incidentally, it wasn't easy to dress the couple, for although the bride could be a child mannequin, even store models are larger today in stature than gentlemen were in 1800, and a great deal of ingenuity had to be used in making the clothes fit. A large wedding cake was placed on the side table, and festive greens and garlands decorated the room.

On another occasion the decorations of the Federal Parlor took their theme from the Adam-style carving over the fireplace, and from the delicate pink color in the wallpaper. Now the room is decorated for a formal ball (photo #47, page 50). Pretty pink ribbon bows are over the fireplace, cleverly wired so that they stand out to repeat the mantel carving. Roses are everywhere: small five-petal hedge roses, and charming little pink multipetaled roses so perfect that one feels like going near to smell them. Pink roses decorate a Queen Anne's Lace wreath (photo #65, page 96). A decanter of wine is placed on the sideboard, and a dish of marzipan is decorative as well as mouth-watering (photo #46, page 50).

THE EMPIRE PERIOD

The last room in our tour dates from about 1825 and is called the Empire Room because its decor was strongly influenced in style by the French Empire. Although there is a return to the Greek classical form, the furniture is sturdier and more elaborate. Ceilings at this time were higher. The fireplace (photo #49, page 51) has a coal grate, indicating the last word in efficiency. The mantel came from the old Paul Revere Tavern in Lexington. Fortunately for museums, New England people are apt to hang on to their old possessions, and if a thing is not sold, it is stored in the attic. The wallpaper in this room had been stored unused for many years in a Concord attic and was a real find, for it was just right for the Empire Room. The French clock on the mantel was bought at the auction of the effects of Joseph Boneparte, who lived in America from 1815 to 1832. Its decorations of a lion and eagle, alabaster columns, and drapery swags are all characteristic of the period. The sofa (photo #50, page 51) with its gracefully scrolled arms and classic proportions was the property of the Reverend Ezra Ripley, minister in Concord from 1778 to 1841, and stood in his parlor at the Old Manse. Ripley was the successor of the Reverend William Emerson, who died of camp fever contracted at Fort Ticonderoga, where he was a chaplain during the Revolution.

Ripley also succeeded in the Widow Emerson's affections. When the couple was about to marry, however, there was a great deal of criticism among the parishioners, for the bride was a decade older than the groom. Ripley was a match for them; tradition has it that he sent word that there would be no weddings or funerals in Concord until such talk stopped. The people thought that over and decided that, after all, there was not so great an age difference; so the couple married and lived happily in the Old Manse with their large family of Emersons and Ripleys. There is a charming silhouette (not pictured) of Ezra Ripley on the wall of the Empire Room, for he was a gentleman of the old school and the last man in town to wear knee breeches. The next to last was the town clerk, Dr. Abiel Heywood. There is an oft-told tale of Heywood's approaching nuptials when he was in his sixties. He decided to wear for the occasion his first pair of pantaloons, meaning long trousers. The only problem was, as he confided to one of the town wits, he wasn't sure how to put them on. The town wit promptly replied that he understood they were put on over the head.

At last in this room we have come to the period of the Christmas tree, for this is the Victorian time. In *Godey's Lady Book* in 1850, there was a picture of the Christmas tree that Queen Victoria and Prince Albert had in the castle for their children. The Christmas tree is of German origin, and at about this time a German member of the Follen Church in East Lexington decorated a Christmas tree for the children of the parish, which was the first public tree in New England. The Follen Church prides itself on being the Christmas Tree Church. If the royal family sanctioned decorations for Christmas, Americans were not slow to follow. The tree in the Empire Room is decorated with small wooden toys and baubles, with of course an angel on top (photo #51, page 51). A Christmas wreath hangs on the back of an armchair (photo #52, page 52). Victorian-style toys as well as Christmas packages not yet opened are under the tree. In the small paned window hang prisms, each attached with a red ribbon bow (photo #53, page 52). The table is set for a party with molded and tinted ice cream in flower shapes, each nestling in a bed of spun sugar. Over the mantel, and highlighting the gold in the wallpaper, is a wreath of gilded lemon leaves (photo #49, page 51). This kind of decoration was described in *Godey's Lady Book*.

In spite of the fact that the people in Concord in years past did not celebrate Christmas as we do today, it was a very special day, and they all flocked to the meetinghouse for a service. The First Parish was not only the only church in Concord for two hundred years, it was the only meeting place as well. Town meetings were held there, as were the First and Second Provincial Congresses at which Sam Adams and John Hancock gave impassioned pleas to resist England's despotic rule. During the days of the Revolutionary War, when the British held Cambridge, Harvard College moved to Concord and held classes in the church. No wonder it was called the meetinghouse. It is particularly appropriate that on one of the days of An Olde Concord Christmas a luncheon has been served in the vestry of the meetinghouse. Since it is a short distance from the Museum, most people prefer to walk, but some choose to ride in the old farm wagon. The master of the riding stable drives the two great farm horses, and for the occasion he wears his tall silk hat and bright red coat. A jovial soul, he soon has his passengers singing "Jingle Bells" as the wagon moves slowly through the village. It is fun to see well-dressed gentlemen and mink-clad ladies sitting on bales of hay, singing their hearts out for Christmas.

As we look back over the years, we realize that the observance of Christmas has changed dramatically. What started out as a strong religious conviction that celebrating Christmas in any way except church-going was blasphemous became for many years only a custom, and finally changed entirely. In his earlier years Henry Thoreau celebrated Christmas by taking a walk, which he did every day. He did write in his journal how one time he stopped to look at the gifts displayed in the window of Wright's Tavern, but they were New Year presents according to custom. On Christmas Day Bronson Alcott, sitting in his lonely study, was greatly cheered by a visit from his friend Ralph Waldo Emerson. Later, as the celebration of Christmas changed, the Alcott family decorated their house and exchanged gifts. The guides at the Alcott house this year reproduced the family's Christmas celebration as it appears in the first chapter of *Little Women*. Sprigs of greens tied with red bows were distributed through the house, a Christmas tree stood in the corner of the parlor, and on the center table were gifts from the girls to their beloved Marmee. In the dining room the table was set for Christmas breakfast, the very meal they were not to have, for they gave it to a poor family. In the kitchen were breads, pies, and gingerbread men, and the oven door was ajar to show the beanpot. Upstairs in the playroom a little wooden sled was tied with a large red ribbon.

Today Concord celebrates Christmas in its usual thorough manner. Along the Lexington Road the 1714 inn stands at the head of the street, and the two churches face each other near the common. All the houses have a white candle in every window, for this represents the religious aspect of the season. The business district is ablaze with lights in the stores, and on the street, the light poles are graced with laurel ropes with white lights. On one evening before

Christmas all the stores are open for shoppers; punch, coffee, or hot mulled cider, along with cookies, is served. Bell ringers and groups of carolers roam the streets. Hayrides are available, and of course Santa Claus is on hand.

Most houses have a wreath or swag on the door, as do the churches, stores, town houses, and hospital. Although the historic houses are closed for the season, loving hands remember to place a wreath on the door of the Old Manse, the Alcott house, and the home of Ralph Waldo Emerson. Some people tie a swag of greens with a red bow to the street-sign pole nearest their home. Many of the towns have Messiah sings, where the people come with their own copies of the score. There is an orchestra, soloists, and a director. When the director raises his baton, the entire audience stands; and when they sing out on those familiar choruses, it is something wonderful to hear. The hospital waiting rooms and corridors are decorated, and patients in nursing homes receive a bowl of berries or a plant, or a dish of bulbs given and distributed by the garden club. On Christmas Day, you may even see some of the townspeoples' dogs with red ribbon bows on their collars.

On Christmas Eve the townspeople gather around the town Christmas tree for a carol sing, and so many come that the common is packed. Then the various churches have services.

It is easy to see that with all the activities of the season already enjoyed, Christmas Day with its family gatherings, opening of gifts, and traditional turkey dinner is just the finishing touch of a glorious Christmas in Concord.

3. Decoration by Mrs. Peter A. Brooke, Mrs. W. Lawrence Marshall, Jr., and Mrs. Marshall Simonds.

Joanna Stetson

4. Decoration by Mrs. Roswell M. Boutwell III, Mrs. Francis A. Houston, and Mrs. Harvey Wheeler.

Nanlee Smith

5. Decoration by Mrs. Robert M. Armstrong and Mrs. Jacque R. Smith.

3. *Top.* The Seventeenth-Century House (1685). As you enter the house, dim light from the tiny leaded windows makes it just possible to see an interior constructed with no frills—the furnishings are simple and sturdy—but there is a cherished piece of Turkey carpet on the table. A glow from the fireplace reminds us that this was the most important area of the home.

4. *Lower left.* The Seventeenth-Century Room (*c.* 1690–1700). We move to another seventeenth-century interior, this one showing the hall of a more prosperous settler in the area, where celebrations of an abundant harvest are portrayed. Most of the furnishings in this room are in the Elizabethan tradition, some with elaborately carved decorations.

5. *Lower right.* Despite the sober Puritan view of life and the rigors of a pioneering existence, an air of festivity and Thanksgiving permeated the life style following harvest time. Beside the open Bible is a sprig of partridgeberry and on the storage chests beyond are simple refreshments. A rundlet, a small cask used by farmers to carry rum, can be seen on the window ledge behind.

6. *Decoration by Mrs. Robert M. Armstrong and Mrs. Jacque R. Smith.*

7. *Decoration by Mrs. Roswell M. Boutwell III, Mrs. Francis A. Houston, and Mrs. Harvey Wheeler.*

6. *Top.* The earliest colonists in Concord survived on a basic diet of Indian corn, squash, pumpkins, wild game, and fish from the Concord rivers. Apples and other fruits were added in time, as well as many vegetables and even delicacies such as turtle soup, for huge turtles lived near the rivers then, just as they do today.

7. *Bottom.* Typical of most seventeenth-century Concord homes, the Museum's Seventeenth-Century Room fireplace has no oven, so the baking was done in heavy pots. Golden rounds of cornbread baked over smoldering embers made tempting and filling fare, and johnnycake on a hearth was a common —and beautiful—sight. Indians taught the early settlers many uses of corn, a food unknown to the settlers when they arrived in New England.

8. Decoration by Mrs. Joyce Webster.

9. Decoration by Mrs. Bruce K. Nelson.

8. *Top*. When her husband had brought home a deer, one of the ways the housewife preserved some of it was in the form of minced meat. To make a pie, she would combine it with suet, quince, juniper berries, honey, lemon juice, raisins, and various herbs and pepper. (Note the pepper masher.) The crock on the table is full of oak leaves to be used for another project: to line potholders.

9. *Middle*. One year, as visitors left the Seventeenth-Century Room, a few of the smaller ones spotted a mouse quietly enjoying its own special feast of dried beans on the floor under a storage chest.

10. *Bottom*. In the midst of a series of trade signs on the walls of the passageway leading to rooms of a later period is a weathered tin sign. It provided the motif for the Museum's very first "Time of Christmas," when the members of the Garden Club of Concord created for each period room a holiday scene in keeping with its time in history.

10.

11. Decoration by Mrs. Clifton Owens, Jr.

12.

13. Decoration by Mrs. Richard E. Hale.

11. *Top left.* The Pine-Ceiled Room (*c.* 1700). Very few extra touches marked the holiday season for the hard-working family who lived here. It is a warm and friendly spot where the products of the family's own hands add gentle beauty to the simple room. Brightly polished apples from their own trees and brown-shelled eggs from their precious hens gleam in the subdued light.

12. *Top right.* To facilitate the job of cleaning in seventeenth-century homes, a pattern was swept into the sand-covered floor every morning, and occasionally the sand was sifted to eliminate the larger particles. Sand spread on the floor also provided a form of insulation.

13. *Bottom.* The Crane Room (early eighteenth century). The welcoming fireplace with its great iron crane beckoned to family and friends alike. The pipe rack hanging in the fireplace was used to purify pipes, which were passed from person to person. A garland of arborvitae, ferns, milkweed pods, and wheat above an unused fireplace of this period can be an attractive decoration at Christmas.

Bruce K. Nelson

14. Decoration by Mrs. Richard E. Hale.

Louise M. Johnson

15.

Bruce K. Nelson

16. Decoration by Mrs. William F.A. Stride.

14. *Top.* A penny shop! Here, in the bay window of the Crane Room, are all sorts of toys and goodies of long ago. In New England, as in the homeland, the shopkeepers started their stores in their homes. These stores became as much a center for social activities as for buying and selling.

15. *Bottom left.* This lantern is one of two that Paul Revere arranged to have hung from the steeple of the Old North Church on the night of April 18, 1775, to inform the patriots that the British were on the move. It was sold by the sexton in 1782 to Daniel Brown of Concord, whose grandson gave it to Cummings E. Davis in 1853.

16. *Bottom right.* The original picture of the scene, painted by Ralph Earle only three months after the April 19, 1775, battle, is a reminder of Concord's part in the Revolution. The Relic Room, where this picture hangs, serves as a gallery and passageway, so no attempt is made to decorate it in "period" fashion. Instead, today's traditional Christmas flowers pick up the colors in the painting.

17. Decoration by Mrs. Bruce K. Nelson and Mrs. John W. Teele.

18. Decoration by Mrs. George Erie and Mrs. David D. Tuttle.

17. *Top.* The Green Room (*c.* 1710–40). We imagine a genial host, against a background of fine paneling, urging friends to share his board and pass around the posset pot, which, in the English tradition, served as a loving cup on Christmas Eve.

18. *Bottom.* Trade with the Orient brought tea and spices to New England, with porcelain sometimes serving as ballast in the holds of clipper ships. In 1822 a Concord family received this set of china, decorated in gold and orange hues, and we imagine a memorable Christmas Eve dinner with the Green Room as its background. Bayberries and Russian olive branches rest on the greens and velvet ribbons that crisscross the table.

19. Decoration by Mrs. George Erie.

20. Decoration by Mrs. Mary Cobb, Mrs. S. Kenneth Neill, and Mrs. W. Ward Willett.

19. *Top.* On the lowboy, delicious foods wait: cranberry bread to be served with the roast goose, a compote of cherries and candied ginger, a Christmas plum pudding, and, to everyone's delight, a rumball and greens tree.

20. *Bottom.* On another occasion, the Jacobean table is ready for relatives arriving by sleigh from Boston. The countryside has been blanketed with snow, and the hungry travelers will be greeted with mugs of hot mulled cider. Later there will be a supper of steaming hot chowder, crusty bread, and cheese. A festive touch is given to the table with clusters of red berries circling the candles.

Nanlee Smith

21. *Decoration by Mrs. Richard Ferraro, Mrs. Robert B. Johnson, Mrs. Stephen Verrill, and Mrs. E.J. Zurlo.*

Nanlee Smith

22. *Decoration by Mrs. Richard Ferraro, Mrs. Robert B. Johnson, Mrs. Stephen Verrill, and Mrs. E.J. Zurlo.*

Bruce K. Nelson

23. *Decoration by Mrs. Paul R. Dinsmore.*

21. *Top.* The Queen Anne Room (*c.* 1740–60). The homes of Concord families in the eighteenth century were not as austere as those of the early settlers. The furnishings of the Queen Anne Room are comfortable, and its harp spinet and tea table indicate that music and social niceties played a larger part in their lives than in the seventeenth century. In some homes, in spite of the 1750 ban on theatre groups, strolling puppeteers were even invited to entertain family and friends.

22. *Bottom left.* For a holiday party, the tea table, specially made to serve the newly introduced tea, is set with an assortment of sweets: molasses cake, mince tarts, and jumbals (a sweet cookie flavored with brandy, cinnamon, or mace).

23. *Bottom right.* An extra music rack was needed when there was a large gathering of musical friends and not everyone could see the music propped on the spinet. We decorated it for the occasion with clusters of lady apples perched on branches of fragrant juniper.

Nanlee Smith

24. Decoration by Mrs. David K. Johnson and Mrs. Albert C. Lesneski.

Nanlee Smith

25. Decoration by Mrs. David K. Johnson and Mrs. Albert C. Lesneski.

24. *Top.* After a festive holiday dinner, the gentlemen may have retired to the Queen Anne Room for a congenial game of cards. Although games and gambling were frowned upon in these early days of the colonies, many indulged themselves in the privacy of their own homes. A game table is ready for play with Chinese ivory gambling counters and cards, while a cheery fire across the room will warm the players.

25. *Bottom.* Over the fireplace a large garland is suspended from the ceiling molding with soft yellow velvet ribbons. The materials used: boxwood and artemisia decorated with lemons, yellow day lilies, feverfew, yarrow, daisies, and canterbury bells. A Hogarth curve arrangement on the harp spinet follows the theme and texture of the garland.

26. Decoration by Mrs. S. Willard Bridges, Jr. and Mrs. Peter A. Brooke.

26. The Chippendale Room (*c.* 1760–80). The Chippendale Room reflects the colonies' prosperity before the Revolution. Local craftsmen, inspired by Thomas Chippendale's elegant designs, produced fine pieces for Concord homes. At the same time, stylish goods and furnishings were imported from Europe and the Orient. Delft tiles, surmounted here by a decoration of strawflowers, grapes, and woodland fruits, typify the desire to be in vogue.

27. *Decoration by Mrs. Peter A. Brooke.*

28. *Decoration by Mrs. Pierce B. Browne.*

29. *Decoration by Mrs. Pierce B. Browne.*

30. *Decoration by Mrs. Mary Cobb.*

27. *Top.* The distinctive puce color of the fireplace tiles is carried throughout the room and has been repeated in restrained decorations for each of our special occasions. On a side table stand the makings of a spicy, hot punch. Even though the family will have carried foot warmers to church on Christmas Eve, we know they will be grateful for the warmth of the punch on their return.

28. *Second from top.* The Pembroke table, which belonged to the Thoreau family, has on it a sumptuous fruit arrangement in a China-trade bowl. Many varieties of fruits were imported to Boston even in the seventeenth century, and for special occasions some must surely have made their way to Concord.

29. *Third from top.* This detail shows pomegranates, apples, grapes, and other fruits used in this arrangement in the China-trade bowl.

30. *Bottom.* On some occasions, wreaths have been hung above the fireplace. Each has contained materials which, when preserved, have the fashionable color so well represented in the room. This wreath is composed of artemisia, pink roses, joe-pye weed and other dried materials. Joe-pye weed is reported to have gotten its name from an Indian named Joe Pye, who urged its use for every conceivable medical need.

31. Decoration by Mrs. John W. Logan and Mrs. Egbert S. Newbury, Jr.

33. Decoration by the Museum Flower Committee.

34. Decoration by Mrs. Barbara Dunfy, Mrs. David Porter, Mrs. G.M. Roddy, and Mrs. James Rothrock.

32. Decoration by Mrs. Joseph E. Dahmen and Mrs. Jacque R. Smith.

31. *Top left.* The Revolutionary Bedroom (*c.* 1775–90). Across the hall from the Chippendale Room is a bed chamber with furnishings also of the Revolutionary period. Here a four-poster bed with freshly turned down sheets, a warming pan tucked between them, awaits a soldier due home from battle for Christmas.

32. *Bottom left.* Our Concord patriot, seated at his desk smoking and attending to correspondence, is still wearing the minuteman's standard garb. This is the original uniform worn by the model for Daniel Chester French's famous sculpture of the Concord minuteman.

33. *Top right.* At the foot of the four-poster bed, a charming nasturtium arrangement graces a tea table that belonged to Dr. John Cuming. (This arrangement is not part of the Museum's Christmas exhibit.) A fine chest on chest, attributed to the Concord cabinetmaker Joseph Hosmer, with the date 1790 carved on the back, can be seen in the candlelight.

34. *Bottom right.* A roundabout chair in the corner invites our soldier to lounge by the fire. The cast-iron fireback, which covers the rear of the fireplace, will reflect more heat into this room than did fireplaces of earlier periods. His family has hung on the paneling above the fireplace greens with ribbons and bittersweet, which repeat the warm tones of the decorative details in this room.

35. Decoration by Mrs. Alan C. Bemis.

36. Decoration by Mrs. Bruce K. Nelson.

37. Decoration by Mrs. Bruce K. Nelson.

35. *Top.* The Hallway. Throughout the year, a tall clock and an arrangement of foliage on a table in the corner of the front hall greet visitors to the Museum. What foliage could be more welcoming at Christmastide than a combination of juniper and pine with the shiny leaves and red berries of holly?

36. *Middle.* On the front door we hang a wreath on the inside, as well as the outside, for these festive occasions. This one was used when the hall was treated with a Victorian motif. Beech leaves form the background with clusters of artificial grapes, swamp grass, and slices of osage orange for decoration. Osage oranges brown when baked and are similar to sections of pine cones.

37. *Bottom.* As we ascend the stairs of the Museum, we pass another tall clock, this one on the landing. The window ledge is deep, and plants or arrangements are pleasing in this area. Red velvet under the Sèvres cache pot draws attention to the red flowers in a mass arrangement of dried flowers that includes: artemisia, larkspur, peonies, oriental poppies, hydrangea, roses, feverfew, foxglove, and lilies.

38. *Decoration by Mrs. Rob Roy McGregor and Mrs. Whitfield Painter, Jr.*

39. *Decoration by Mrs. Rob Roy McGregor and Mrs. Whitfield Painter, Jr.*

40. *Decoration by Mrs. Austin F. Lyne and Mrs. Charles A. Morss, Jr.*

38. *Top left.* The Yellow Room (*c.* 1790–1815). For each year of the series, we treated the bed-chamber at the top of the stairs as a young Victorian girl's room. It gave us an opportunity to display a few of the many dolls and toys from the Museum's storage areas. In 1979 this room was changed into a permanent gallery where toys and examples of nineteenth-century decorative arts are shown.

39. *Top right.* Ribbons are featured in this room, for they were worn by most little girls at that time. Here red ribbons outline the paneling above the mantel and trim a wreath decked with small toys. Another toy, a red crocheted doll, a present to a small friend from Ralph Waldo Emerson, sits on the mantel.

40. *Bottom left.* At the foot of the feather bed is a small table covered with ribbons woven to form a cloth for a dolls' tea party. In the middle of the table a little girl has set a tiny tree trimmed with bows to make the party quite special.

41. Decoration by Mrs. Joyce Webster.

42. Decoration by Mrs. Robert L. Lyon and Mrs. Bruce K. Nelson.

43. Decoration by Mrs. Gerald Lauderdale.

44. Decoration by Mrs. John M. Reynolds III and Mrs. Joyce Webster.

41. *Top left.* The Reeded Room (*c.* 1800). The classical influence of the Adam period is seen in architectural details of the Reeded Room, which gets its name from the carved decoration in the molding. A small example is seen in this mantel detail with its decoration of greens and ribbon.

42. *Top right.* On one occasion, this room was prepared for a Christmas visit by the first granddaughter and her parents. The grandparents brought down from the attic a hobby horse, toys, and a doll to delight the child. Her grandmother made a miniature flower arrangement for the dolls' tea table.

43. *Bottom left.* A pot of hot chocolate and a cranberry cake have been brought to the visiting family's room to refresh them after their journey.

44. *Bottom right.* Another year, the Reeded Room showed the delightful array of dresses to be worn by bridesmaids for the wedding to take place in the Federal Parlor. A tea table is set with decanter, glasses, and fruitcake.

45. Decoration by Mrs. Frank W. Wilson.

46. Decoration by Mrs. Mary Cobb, Mrs. Robert L. Lyon, and Mrs. James Knight.

47. Decoration by Mrs. Mary Cobb and Mrs. James Knight.

48. Decoration by Mrs. Peter A. Brooke, Mrs. S. Willard Bridges, Jr., and Mrs. William F.A. Stride.

45. *Top left.* The Alcove (*c.* 1812). On the desk in the small alcove between the Reeded Room and the Federal Parlor are cloaks, shawls, bonnets, gloves, and a top hat of the period, left as they would have been by guests at any nineteenth-century ball.

46. *Top right.* The Federal Parlor (*c.* 1800-1810). A christening at Christmastide is the excuse for a real celebration. On the pier table between the windows, wine and cookies are ready for the arrival of the guests; the waiting family can be seen in the mirror above the refreshment table.

47. *Bottom left.* The classical garland used as an architectural feature under the mantel of the Federal Parlor is echoed above by a garland of ivy, carnations, and pink ribbons.

48. *Bottom right.* Here the Federal Parlor is decorated with ivy and roses for a holiday wedding reception. The bride in her silk brocaded wedding dress holds a bouquet of roses.

49. Decoration by Mrs. Richard E. Hale.   *50.*

51. Decoration by Mrs. Richard E. Hale.

49. *Top left.* The Empire Room (*c.* 1825). Classical motifs and forms became heavy in the Empire period. This weightiness is reflected in the gilded leaves that form the wreath and in the garland decorating the fireplace wall.

50. *Top right.* Seated on the Empire-style sofa, which belonged to the Reverend Ezra Ripley, minister in Concord from 1778 to 1841, is a mannequin wearing a dress owned by Louisa May Alcott, Concord authoress of *Little Women.* Louisa's rag doll, made by her mother for Louisa's seventh birthday, looks on from the corner of the sofa.

51. *Bottom.* The Empire Room is the setting for our Victorian Christmases, and in this room, for the first time, we can properly show a Christmas tree lavishly decorated in the German manner. Modeled on the first Christmas tree used in New England, this one is decorated with shiny balls, tiny wax tapers, gilded egg shells, cornucopias filled with candy, and toys and whimsies.

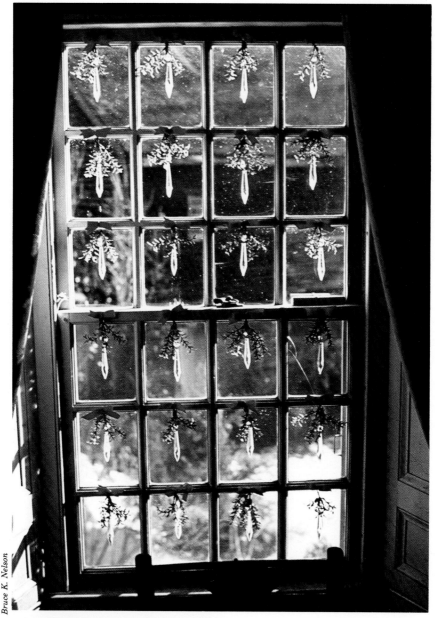

Bruce K. Nelson

53. Decoration by Mrs. Richard E. Hale.

Bruce K. Nelson

52. Decoration by Mrs. Bruce K. Nelson and Mrs. Harvey Wheeler.

52. *At left.* A tableau suggested by a William Frith painting reflects the tastes and customs of the late Victorians. A wreath of flowers on a high chair (and a birthday cake on a crystal stand) leaves little doubt that the room is the scene of a child's birthday party.

53. *Above.* Through this window in the Empire Room, with its glittering prism decoration, we get our final glimpse of the Seventeenth-Century House where our tour began. This is the conclusion of An Olde Concord Christmas.

METRIC MEASURING EQUIVALENTS

FOR COOKING

(nearest approximation for American measures)

LIQUID

1	teaspoon = 5 milliliters
1	tablespoon = 15 milliliters
3	tablespoons + 1 teaspoon = ½ deciliter
6	tablespoons + 2 teaspoons = 1 deciliter
½	cup + 1 teaspoon = 1.25 deciliter (⅛ liter)
¾	cup + 4 teaspoons = 2 deciliters
1	cup + 2 teaspoons = 2.5 deciliters (¼ liter)
2	cups + 4 teaspoons = 5 deciliters (½ liter)
1	quart + 2 tablespoons + 2 teaspoons = 10 deciliters (1 liter)
500	milliliters = 1.06 pints
1	liter = 1.06 quarts
4	liters = 1.06 gallons

DRY

1	ounce = 28.35 grams
3½	ounces = 100 grams
1	pound = 453.58 grams
1	pound, 1½ ounces = 500 grams
2	pounds, 3 ounces = 1 kilogram
30	grams = 1.1 ounces
100	grams = 3.6 ounces
250	grams = 9.0 ounces
500	grams = 1.1 pounds
1	kilogram = 2.2 pounds

A speck or a dash or a pinch is ⅛ teaspoon or less = ¾ milliliter

TRADITIONAL HOLIDAY FOODS AND DECORATIONS

APPETIZERS AND DIPS

RILLETTES OF GOOSE
This is my own recipe.

4 cups leftover roast or braised goose meat
    (without fat, bone, or gristle), cut into ½-
    inch pieces or smaller
2 cups rich goose gravy or excellent broth
½ cup Madeira (optional)
3 cups goose fat (reserved from when goose
    was first cooked)
1 bay leaf
1 teaspoon thyme
salt, if needed, to taste

Put the meat, gravy, Madeira (if used), fat, bay
leaf, and thyme into a heavy kettle. If necessary, add water to bring the level of fat and
liquid to the top of the meat. Bring to a slow
simmer and cook until all the liquid has evaporated—about 5 or 6 hours. Then, monitoring
the process more closely, continue to simmer
the mixture until the meat is a rich brown. Do
not cover pot, but do stir occasionally to prevent the meat from sticking to the bottom and
scorching. Remove from the fire. Drain off
about 1 cup of fat and set it aside. When the
rillettes have cooled, beat them in a mixer or
with a wooden spoon. For taste, add salt, if
needed, and some or all of the reserved fat. The
mixture is supposed to be quite rich, since it is
consumed in small quantities, so all of the remaining cup of fat may be needed. It will keep
for a month or so in the refrigerator. It has the
advantage of being ready to serve as is, without any further preparation.
Yield: 5 cups
Can be frozen; tightly wrapped, it will keep
for up to 6 months with no loss of texture and
little loss of flavor.
Mrs. Robert Wheaton

PÂTÉ MAISON
Best pâté I have ever tasted!

1 pound chicken livers
1 pound lean pork
1 pound sausage meat
1 tablespoon chopped chives or shallots
1 tablespoon chopped parsley
2 teaspoons ground pepper
½ teaspoon ginger
½ teaspoon cinnamon
salt to taste
2 tablespoons brandy
2 tablespoons dry sherry
10 slices bacon

Grind all meat except bacon twice. Add remaining ingredients except bacon and mix well. Line an 8 × 6 × 3-inch loaf pan with bacon (uncooked) and pack in the mixture. Cover with bacon and bake at 350° for 2½ hours. Remove from heat, cover, and weight with a heavy brick on top while cooling. Slice and serve with bread or toast.
Yield: 1 large loaf
Mrs. Frederick C. Livingston

SALAMI SAUSAGE

5 pounds extra lean ground beef chuck
5 teaspoons curing salt
2 teaspoons ground black peppercorns
2½ teaspoons mustard seeds
2½ teaspoons garlic salt
1 teaspoon hickory smoked salt
1 teaspoon celery seed (optional)

Mix all ingredients thoroughly. Refrigerate for three days, kneading once a day. Shape into five rolls, 1½ to 2 inches by 6 inches. Bake at 150° for 10 hours, turning once or twice. Serve with crackers.
Yield: 5 rolls
Can be frozen
Mrs. Leonard Seale

SHRIMP CHEKHOV
During the production of The Three Sisters *at college, this was concocted and immediately christened "Shrimp Chekhov."*

2 tablespoons chopped parsley
2 tablespoons onion
2 tablespoons pimiento
2 tablespoons sweet relish
2 tablespoons green pepper
⅓ cup oil
¼ cup vinegar
salt, pepper, sugar to taste
2 pounds cooked shrimp

Combine all ingredients except shrimp. Add shrimp to mixture and marinate 8 hours or overnight. To serve, put in a shallow bowl to retain marinade. Serve with toothpicks.
Yield: 8–10 servings
Mrs. Robert Williams

SALMON MOUSSE
This is fun to serve with drinks when a fish mold is used and decorated with an olive slice as an eye, pimiento for the mouth, and a parsley ring around the neck.

1 envelope gelatin
¼ cup water
1½ teaspoons salt
1½ teaspoons dry mustard
2 tablespoons granulated sugar
2 eggs
1 cup sour cream
¼ cup white vinegar
1½ cups cooked, boned salmon

Sprinkle gelatin over cold water to soften. In double boiler, mix salt, mustard, sugar, eggs, sour cream, and vinegar. Cook, stirring, until thickened. Remove from heat. Stir in gelatin and dissolve. Pour mixture over salmon, toss, then turn into an oiled 1-quart mold. Refrigerate until set. To serve, spread on bland crackers as an hors d'oeuvres or on a bed of Boston lettuce with a dollop of mayonnaise as a first course.
Yield: 1 quart
Mrs. Frederick M. Fritz

FISH LOG

1 large can salmon
8-ounce carton whipped cream cheese
1 tablespoon minced onion
1 tablespoon lemon juice
1 teaspoon prepared horseradish
dash Tabasco
¼ teaspoon liquid smoke (optional)
½ cup chopped pecans or walnuts
½ cup snipped fresh parsley

Drain and flake salmon. Add remaining ingredients except nuts and parsley; mix well. Refrigerate for 2–3 hours or overnight. Shape

salmon mixture (chilled) into a ball or log. Roll to cover in parsley and nut mixture. Serve with assorted crackers.
Yield: 2 cups
Mrs. Alfred Bertocchi

CHEESE HORS D'OEUVRES

1 cup flour
2 cups grated sharp cheese
½ teaspoon salt
1 teaspoon paprika
¼ pound butter
1 jar pitted green olives

Let ingredients soften to room temperature, then mix thoroughly everything except olives. Flatten out 1 tablespoon of mixture, place green olive in middle and roll into ball in palm of hands. Freeze. Bake frozen at 400° for 15 minutes. (For variation, deviled ham may be substituted for olive.)
Yield: 50 or more
Mrs. Frederick S. Jones, II

MUSHROOM ROLL-UPS

½ pound mushrooms, minced
¼ cup butter
1 cup light cream
3 tablespoons flour
¾ teaspoon salt
2 teaspoons chives
1 teaspoon lemon juice
1 loaf very thinly sliced white bread

Sauté mushrooms in butter. Stir in 1 cup light cream and cook until thick. Add remaining ingredients except bread. Cut crusts off bread. Roll bread with rolling pin until thin. Spread mixture on bread and roll up. Slice in thirds. (Do not cut if you plan to put in freezer.) Bake 10 minutes at 400°. Recipe can be doubled by adding 8 ounces of lobster meat.
Yield: 3½ dozen
Can be frozen
Mrs. John Kris

MARINATED MUSHROOMS

1 pound fresh or 2 6-ounce cans button mushrooms
¼ cup wine vinegar
½ cup olive oil
2 teaspoons chives
¼ clove garlic
¼ teaspoon salt
¼ teaspoon granulated sugar
¼ teaspoon pepper
1 teaspoon lemon juice

Combine all ingredients; marinate overnight. Place in a bowl and serve with toothpicks.
Yield: Approximately 75 mushrooms
Mrs. Allen Mottur

BROCCOLI SANDWICHES

1 bunch broccoli
⅓ cup mayonnaise
1 tablespoon lemon juice
salt to taste
bread

Using very green and very fresh broccoli, chop only the flowerets very finely. Mix the raw broccoli with mayonnaise, lemon juice, and salt to taste. Spread the mixture on fresh bread rounds cut small for hors d'oeuvres or larger for tea sandwiches.
Yield: 40 small rounds
Mrs. Floyd Verrill

SPINACH SQUARES

4 tablespoons butter or margarine
3 eggs
1 cup flour
1 cup milk
1 teaspoon salt
1 teaspoon baking powder
1 pound mild cheddar, grated
20 ounces cooked spinach, drained and chopped
1 tablespoon chopped onion (optional)
seasoned salt (optional)

Preheat oven to 350°. Put butter in 9 × 13 × 2-inch baking dish and melt in oven. Remove. In a large bowl beat eggs well, then add flour, milk, salt, and baking powder. Mix well. Add cheese, spinach, and onion (if used). Again, mix well. Spoon into baking dish and level off. Sprinkle with seasoned salt, if desired. Bake at 350° for 35 minutes. Remove and let cool 45 minutes, then cut into bite-size squares ¾ inch to 1 inch each. If frozen, defrost and reheat at 325° for 12 minutes.
Yield: 40 to 60 squares
Can be frozen
Mrs. Nathaniel Bates

FESTIVE CRAB DIP

8 ounces cream cheese
1 tablespoon milk
1 6½-ounce can flaked crabmeat or fresh
*   equivalent*
1 teaspoon cream-style horseradish (or more
*   if you like it hotter, and depending on the*
*   kind of crabmeat you use. Fresh crabmeat*
*   tends to be more bland than canned)*
¼ teaspoon salt
dash Worchestershire sauce
dash pepper
1 medium onion, chopped

paprika (optional)
toasted slivered almonds (optional)

Blend together cheese and milk; add crabmeat and remaining ingredients. Place in a small casserole and bake at 350° for 15 minutes or until bubbly on top. May be sprinkled with paprika and/or topped with toasted slivered almonds. Best served with bland crackers.
Yield: 6–8 servings
Mrs. Joseph T. McColgan, Jr.

VEGETABLE DIP

¾ cup real mayonnaise
3 ounces soft cream cheese
1 cup sour cream
1 tablespoon minced onion
1 teaspoon parsley
½ teaspoon Beau Monde (Spice Islands) sea-
*   soning*
½ teaspoon dill weed
¼ teaspoon curry

Combine all ingredients, mix well, and refrigerate 48 hours. Serve with raw vegetables (cauliflower, broccoli, celery, carrots, and cherry tomatoes) cut into bite-size pieces.
Yield: 2½ cups dip
Mrs. Richard Young

SOUPS

TANGY JELLIED CONSOMMÉ

2 cans beef consommé
3 tablespoons lemon juice
pepper to taste
¼ cup tomato juice
2 tablespoons Worcestershire sauce
6 ounces crabmeat
6 teaspoons mayonnaise
curry to taste

Combine first five ingredients. Jell in refrigerator for 4 or 5 hours at least, or overnight. At serving time, place cooked crabmeat at bottom of soup bowl, and spoon consommé on top. Gar-

nish with heaping teaspoon of mayonnaise seasoned with curry.
Yield: 6 servings
Mrs. William B. Moses, Jr.

CAULIFLOWER SOUP
This is also good with broccoli and asparagus.

1 head cauliflower
1 small onion, chopped
¼ cup butter
¼ cup flour
3 cups chicken broth

2 cups milk
1 cup sharp cheese, grated

Cook cauliflower in a small amount of boiling water until tender. Drain and chop coarsely, then set aside. In a large pot, sauté the onion in the butter until the onion is soft and transparent. Blend in the flour; then slowly add the chicken broth, beating with a wire whisk. Add milk. Cook until mixture thickens slightly, stirring constantly. Add cauliflower. Stir in the grated cheese. When cheese melts and soup is hot, it is ready to serve.
Yield: 6 servings
Mrs. Howard Harrison

CHERRY SOUP

1 1-pound can water-pack red sour pitted
 cherries with the liquid
¼ cup granulated sugar
2 teaspoons cornstarch
¼ teaspoon salt
¼ teaspoon cinnamon
2 strips orange peel
½ cup orange juice
½ cup red wine

Combine all ingredients except wine in blender. Cover and blend on high speed for 20 seconds. Pour into saucepan and cook over medium heat, stirring until blended and mixture boils. Remove from heat and stir in red wine. Serve hot or chilled with sour cream.
Yield: 3 servings
Mrs. Earl F. Bracker

PRESIDENTIAL FISH CHOWDER
During the holiday period, when we serve so much turkey, ham, and other meats, I like to prepare this chowder as a change of pace. It is truly elegant.

2½ pounds haddock fillets
2 cups water
¼ pound butter
1¾ cups sliced onions
1 cup chopped celery
2 tablespoons flour

2½ cups peeled and cubed potatoes
1 bay leaf
2½ teaspoons salt
¼ teaspoon pepper
4 cups milk
1 cup medium cream
1 cup sour cream

Simmer fish in water 5 minutes or until it flakes. Remove fish to platter. In large pan, melt 5 tablespoons butter, add onions and celery, and sauté until clear. Stir in flour and gradually add the fish broth. Add potatoes, bay leaf, salt, pepper, and 1 cup finely flaked fish. Simmer, covered, for 20 minutes or until potatoes are tender. Meanwhile, slowly heat milk to scalding. Remove from heat and add cream and sour cream. Beat gently until well combined. Reheat slowly until just hot—not boiling. Add to potato mixture. Heat 5 minutes. Remove bay leaf. Top each serving with remaining butter.
Yield: 3½ quarts (8–10 servings)
Mrs. Frederick Van Veen

OYSTER SOUP
An old family recipe which can be served with Thanksgiving or Christmas dinner.

1 pint oysters, cooked in juice until edges
 curl
3 tablespoons butter
3 tablespoons flour
2 cups milk
salt, pepper, nutmeg, Worcestershire sauce
 to taste
2 tablespoons pimiento, puréed
¼ cup heavy cream, whipped

Mince cooked oysters in blender. Melt butter, stir in flour and milk and bring to boiling point. Add oysters to flour and milk sauce. Flavor with salt, pepper, nutmeg, and Worcestershire sauce. Top with puréed pimiento, which has been mixed into the whipped cream. If desired, add light cream to soup to make right consistency.
Yield: 4 servings
Mrs. E. S. Newbury, Jr.

LENTIL SOUP

1 pound dried lentils
3 quarts water
2 pounds smoked pork hocks
2 medium onions, coarsely chopped
2 tablespoons chopped parsley
1 clove garlic, minced
salt and ground pepper to taste

Combine all ingredients. Bring to a boil, then reduce heat and let simmer for about 2 hours. Remove hocks and set aside. Pick off all meat and chop coarsely. Purée the remaining soup in blender or food mill. Put meat pieces into puréed soup and serve.
Yield: 3 quarts (8 servings)
Mrs. Juris Udris

PARSLEY SOUP

6 tablespoons butter
6 tablespoons flour
5½ cups homemade soup stock of your choice
1 clove garlic, crushed
1 cup parsley, chopped and packed down into
    measuring cup
½ cup sour cream
salt and ground pepper to taste

Heat the butter. Add flour and cook 5 minutes, stirring occasionally. Add stock and simmer, skimming off the scum which forms on the top, for about 10 minutes. Add the garlic and parsley; simmer 1 minute longer. Cover and let stand 15 minutes. Correct the seasoning and reheat before serving. Garnish with a dollop of sour cream. This may be served chilled in the summer.
Yield: 6 servings
Mrs. Harvey Wheeler

BEEF, LAMB, VEAL, AND HAM

BEEF STEW PROVENÇAL
This is a combination of an old French recipe and a Down-East version of beef stew, giving a nice country flavor. A little unusual and easy!

2 pounds beef stew meat, cubed
4–5 carrots, quartered
1 cup chopped celery
4 medium onions
1 whole onion stuck with 4 whole cloves
4 shallots
4 large tomatoes, quartered
1 cup tomato sauce
1 clove garlic, crushed
3 tablespoons minute tapioca
1 cup Burgundy wine
salt, pepper, thyme, parsley to taste
3 bay leaves
pinch cinnamon
rind of half an orange, cut in fine julienne
    strips
1 cup (or more) water chestnuts
1 cup whole mushrooms

Combine all ingredients except chestnuts and mushrooms in a heavy casserole dish, cover, cook in 250° oven for 5 hours. During last hour, add the water chestnuts and the mushrooms. Serve with rice or buttered noodles and grated cheese.
Yield: 6–8 servings
Can be frozen
Mrs. Stephen P. Baldwin

STEAK AND KIDNEY PIE

2 pounds very lean beef chuck
1 pound lamb kidneys
1 large onion
1½ tablespoons bacon fat or oil
1 cup rich beef stock
1 teaspoon Worcestershire sauce
½ tablespoon grated nutmeg
salt, pepper, cayenne to taste
1 flaky pie crust

Remove all fat from beef and cut into 1-inch cubes. Quarter kidneys lengthwise and crosswise. Coarsely chop the onion and brown in bacon fat (or oil) in large frying pan. When onion becomes translucent, add beef cubes and kidneys, stirring constantly until brown on all sides. Add cup of rich beef stock, season to taste with salt, pepper, cayenne, nutmeg, and Worcestershire sauce. Stir well and cover tightly; simmer for 2 hours or until meat is tender. Place meat and juices in a shallow earthenware casserole and cool. When cool, cover with a flaky pie crust. Make several air vents in the crust. Bake 10 minutes at 425°, then reduce oven temperature to 350°. Continue baking another 15 to 20 minutes until the crust is a golden brown. Serve with tiny boiled parsley potatoes, broiled tomatoes, and a crisp green salad.
Yield: 6 servings
Mrs. Peter A. Brooke

VEAL BIRDS IN CASSEROLE

12 veal cutlets
salt, ground pepper, nutmeg, thyme to taste
1 pound seasoned sausage meat
1 cup dry white wine
12 tiny pearl onions, precooked
12 baby carrots
2 tablespoons shortening
2 dozen fresh mushrooms
parsley

Place veal cutlets on a damp surface and season with salt, pepper, nutmeg, and thyme. Pound seasoned cutlets to an even thinness with wooden rolling pin. Place scoop of sausage meat in the center of each cutlet and roll carefully, securing with wooden toothpicks. Brown veal birds on all sides in a little shortening (about 1 tablespoon) in a frying pan. Remove birds to casserole, pour off excess fat, and deglaze pan with wine. Pour pan drippings over birds. Rinse frying pan and dry.

Brown onions and carrots lightly in 1 tablespoon shortening, add mushrooms, and continue cooking for 2 more minutes. Add vegetables to the casserole, sprinkle with parsley, and

season to taste. Cover *tightly* and bake in 325° oven for 1 hour. If more liquid is needed at this point, add some rich beef or veal stock and thicken gravy as you wish. Reheat for 10 to 15 minutes. May be prepared ahead and reheated. Serve with plain rice, a tossed salad, and French bread.
Yield: 6 servings
Mrs. Peter A. Brooke

ORANGE-RAISIN STUFFED LAMB ROLL WITH ORANGE-MINT SAUCE

6-pound leg of lamb, boned and butterflied
salt and pepper to taste
⅔ cup chopped onion
⅔ cup chopped celery
3 tablespoons butter or margarine
4½ cups cubed cinnamon-raisin bread (6 slices)
2 tablespoons grated orange peel
1 beaten egg

Pound lamb to a thickness of ½ to ¾ inch, then sprinkle with salt and pepper. Cook onion and celery in butter or margarine until tender. Toss mixture with bread, orange peel, and egg. Spread mixture over lamb; roll up, jelly-roll fashion, and tie with a string. Cook at 325° for 2½ hours or until meat thermometer registers 170°.

ORANGE-MINT SAUCE
⅓ cup packed brown sugar
2 tablespoons cornstarch
1 teaspoon salt
¾ teaspoon ginger
1¾ cups orange juice
1 tablespoon grated orange peel
2 teaspoons dried mint flakes
2 tablespoons butter
2 oranges, peeled, sectioned, and cut in pieces

Cook all ingredients except butter and oranges and stir until bubbly. Stir in butter and oranges.
Yield: 12 servings
Mrs. Everett Parker

HAM MOUSSE
This is a useful lunch or supper dish when you have some ham left over from a joint.

½ pint stock
1 tablespoon gelatin
1 pound ham, minced
½ cup mayonnaise
½ cup heavy cream, whipped
1 teaspoon Angostura bitters
1 tablespoon chutney

garlic salt
freshly ground pepper

Dissolve gelatin in hot stock and let it set a little. Put ham in bowl. Add mayonnaise, cream, bitters, chutney, garlic salt, and lots of pepper. When gelatin is beginning to set, add to ham mixture. Rinse a mold in cold water, put mixture in, and place in the refrigerator overnight. Turn out and garnish.
Yield: 4–6 servings
Mrs. Richard Vokey

POULTRY

HOT CHICKEN SALAD

2 cups chicken, cooked and cubed
2 cups diced celery
1 cup toasted bread cubes
½ cup toasted almonds
½ teaspoon salt
2 teaspoons grated onion
2 tablespoons lemon juice
1 cup mayonnaise

TOPPING:
½ cup bread cubes
½ cup grated cheese

Combine the chicken, celery, bread cubes, almonds, salt, and onion. Add the mayonnaise and lemon juice and mix well. Pile the mixture lightly into individual baking dishes. Sprinkle the chicken salad with the cheese and bread crumb topping. Bake at 450° for 12 minutes.
Yield: 6 servings
Mrs. David Borrow

CHICKEN SALAD
We used this for the Emerson Hospital fashion show luncheon. It is just great for a large group. The pineapple and almonds give it an extra zing.

10 chicken breasts or 9 pounds chicken meat
1 cup chopped scallions

dash of pepper
2 bay leaves
6 cups chopped celery
½ cup Italian salad dressing
1½ cups chicken broth
2 teaspoons salt
1½ cups sliced almonds
3 cans pineapple chunks, drained
3 cups mayonnaise
6 hard-cooked eggs
lettuce
paprika

Boil chicken with scallions, pepper, and bay leaves until tender. Remove chicken from pot after cooking. Dice chicken. Add celery, dressing, chicken broth, salt, and almonds. Let stand for 3 hours or overnight. Drain any excess liquid. Add pineapple and mayonnaise. Toss and serve on a bed of lettuce. Arrange the hard-cooked eggs on lettuce. Sprinkle with paprika.
Yield: 25 servings
Mrs. Roy O. Harvey

CHICKEN CRÊPES

2 onions, minced
½ green pepper, chopped finely
5 stalks celery, diced
3 tablespoons butter
½ pound mushrooms, thinly sliced

*3 pounds cooked chicken or leftover chicken
or turkey*

BATTER:
*1 cup milk
2 eggs
2 tablespoons melted butter
½ cup flour
½ teaspoon salt*

CHEESE SAUCE:
*1 tablespoon butter
1 tablespoon flour
1½ cups milk
1 cup grated cheddar cheese
salt and pepper to taste*

Lightly brown the onions, green pepper, and celery in butter. Add the mushrooms and simmer 3 minutes, stirring constantly. Cut chicken in ¼-inch cubes and add to vegetables. Season to taste.

To prepare the batter, beat the milk, eggs, and melted butter together. Add flour and salt. Beat until smooth.

To cook the crêpes, lightly butter a small iron frying pan. Pour a little of the batter in the warm pan, tilting the pan so batter is spread evenly all over the bottom. Brown batter on one side over medium heat. Slide crêpe onto a cloth, the light side against the cloth. Place some of the meat and vegetable mixture on each crêpe. Roll. Place crêpes in a casserole side by side. Cover with the cheese sauce. Bake at 300° for 45 minutes. When ready to serve, place crêpes under the broiler for a few minutes to brown.
*Yield: 6 servings
Can be frozen
Mrs. Arthur B. Stetson*

CHICKEN TARRAGON

*1 tablespoon tarragon
1 cup dry white wine
4 tablespoons butter
¼ to ½ cup small button mushrooms
2 chicken breasts, split, skinned, and boned*

*½ pint whipping cream
salt and pepper to taste*

Let tarragon steep in wine for 30 minutes. Sauté mushrooms in butter. Remove mushrooms and set aside. Quickly brown chicken in butter on all sides; add salt and pepper to taste. Cover and slowly cook for 5 minutes or until juices run clear. Transfer chicken to warm platter. Add wine-tarragon mixture to skillet. Cook over high heat until most of wine disappears. Add cream. Heat and simmer for 1 minute. Return mushrooms and chicken to skillet. Heat thoroughly. May be made ahead and reheated. When doubling recipe, no need to double wine and tarragon.
*Yield: 3–4 servings
Mrs. John R. McAllister*

CHICKEN SAUTÉ AU CITRON

*3 large chicken breasts, halved and boned
3 tablespoons butter
juice of 2 oranges
grated rind of 1 orange
grated rind of 1 lemon
3 tablespoons dry sherry
¾ cup light cream
¼ teaspoon salt*

Brown the chicken breasts in the butter, then remove breasts from pan. To pan add remaining ingredients; blend well. Return chicken to pan, spooning sauce over breasts. Cover and cook gently 20 to 25 minutes. Serve over rice.
*Yield: 6 servings
Mrs. Jonathan Keyes*

PHEASANT CASSEROLE WITH CHESTNUTS
This is good for a crowd and a welcome change from the usual roast pheasant!

*1 tablespoon oil
2 tablespoons butter
1 plump pheasant, cleaned
½ pound small white onions, skinned
½ pound fresh chestnuts, peeled and skinned
¼ cup flour*

2 cups chicken stock or broth
½ cup red wine
grated rind and juice of 1 orange
2 teaspoons red currant jelly
1 bay leaf
salt and freshly ground pepper
chopped parsley

Heat oil in frying pan. Add butter and brown pheasant all over. Cut pheasant into serving pieces and place in casserole. Add onions and chestnuts to pan and cook until golden brown.

Transfer to casserole. Add flour to frying pan and cook for 1 minute before whisking in stock, wine, orange rind and juice, and red currant jelly. Bring mixture to a boil, add bay leaf, and season to taste. Pour mixture over pheasant, cover, and cook in moderate oven (325°) for 1½ to 2 hours, until tender. Remove bay leaf and any fat from the juice, adjust seasonings, and garnish with parsley. Serve with wild rice and green salad. Recipe may be doubled.
Yield: 4–6 generous servings
Can be frozen
Mrs. Franklin W. Hobbs

STUFFINGS

CORNBREAD STUFFING
This stuffing has been used by my grandmother, my mother, and myself for many, many years.

1 cup raisins
1½ cups thinly sliced celery
½ cup fresh parsley, chopped
½ cup chopped green onion
¾ cup melted butter
8 cups soft white bread crumbs
6 cups cornbread crumbs
1 cup coarsely chopped salted almonds
1 teaspoon nutmeg
1 teaspoon poultry seasoning
1 teaspoon sage
1 teaspoon salt
½ teaspoon pepper
⅔ cup giblet broth
2 eggs, beaten

Sauté raisins, celery, parsley, and onion in butter. Remove from heat and place in mixing bowl. Add all other ingredients, mixing lightly. Adjust texture (moist or dry) by adding giblet broth. This recipe makes enough stuffing for a large turkey. Leftover stuffing may be placed

in a buttered casserole and baked at 350° for 20 minutes.
Yield: approximately 4–5 quarts
Mrs. Joe B. Wyatt

MRS. H'S TURKEY DRESSING

16 cups coarse bread crumbs
3 cups chopped celery
4 cups coarsely chopped pecans
¾ cup chopped onion
*8 ounces sliced fresh mushrooms, sautéed in
   butter*
2 teaspoons dried basil
salt and pepper to taste
1 pound butter, melted
1 cup milk
½ cup dry white wine

If bread crumbs are soft, dry slightly in oven. In large bowl, combine bread crumbs, celery, pecans, onion, mushrooms, basil, salt, and pepper. Gradually add melted butter, milk, and wine. Toss with fork until well combined.
Yield: enough for 20-pound turkey and some left over
Mrs. Warren H. Oster

FISH AND SEAFOOD

CRAB AND SHERRY CASSEROLE

2 cups crabmeat
2 hard-cooked eggs, chopped
1 cup mayonnaise
1 teaspoon grated onion
1 teaspoon chopped parsley
2 teaspoons lemon juice
½ teaspoon Worcestershire sauce
½ teaspoon prepared mustard
3 tablespoons sherry
1 cup buttered bread crumbs

Mix all ingredients, saving ½ cup bread crumbs to sprinkle on top. Bake at 400° for 15 minutes.
Yield: 6 servings
Mrs. Everett Parker

ESCALLOPED OYSTER CASSEROLE
This recipe belonged to my great-grandmother and was usually served as part of our Christmas Day dinner. It is extremely good.

1 quart oysters
1 quart cracker crumbs
1 cup melted butter
1½ pints milk
salt and pepper to taste

Set aside a few cracker crumbs to sprinkle on top, then combine remaining ingredients in a lightly greased 13 x 9-inch baking dish. Bake 45 minutes to 1 hour in a 375–400° oven. Recipe can be easily cut in half for a small family.
Yield: 8 servings
Mrs. Michael Beer

SEAFOOD CASSEROLE
Sounds like a lot of work, but really isn't!

2 pounds haddock fillets
1 pound lobster meat
8 tablespoons butter
9 tablespoons flour
1 cup evaporated milk
1½ cups whole milk
2 tablespoons cornstarch
2 tablespoons whole milk
1 tablespoon lemon juice
1 tablespoon Worcestershire sauce
1 tablespoon catsup
1 tablespoon horseradish
1 clove garlic, grated
1 teaspoon prepared mustard
½ teaspoon salt
1 teaspoon soy sauce
4 tablespoons minced parsley
¼ cup sherry
bread crumbs
butter

Steam haddock for 20 minutes, cool, then separate into bite-size pieces. Separate lobster into bite-size pieces. Melt butter and blend in flour. Heat evaporated milk with fresh milk and gradually add to flour and butter, stirring constantly. Cook until thick in top of double boiler. Add cornstarch mixed with a little cold milk and cook 10 minutes longer. Add rest of seasonings. Add fish and lobster and pour into greased casserole. Sprinkle top with bread crumbs and dot with butter; bake 30 minutes at 400°. To make a slightly thinner sauce, add extra milk. Then omit bread crumbs and serve mixture over patty shells. A rich and lovely dish for holiday entertaining. May be made a day ahead.
Yield: 8 servings
Mrs. William F. A. Stride

WILD RICE AND SHRIMP CASSEROLE

2 cups wild rice
4 tablespoons butter
1 onion, finely chopped
1 pound mushrooms, thickly sliced
juice of ½ lemon
2 tablespoons flour
1¼ cups chicken stock
½ cup dry white wine
½ teaspoon salt
¼ teaspoon crumbled dried tarragon

⅛ teaspoon white pepper
3 tablespoons grated Gruyère cheese
1½ pounds cooked medium-size shrimp
1 tablespoon finely chopped parsley

Wash and prepare rice as directed on box. Cook in boiling salted water for 25 minutes or until *almost* tender; drain. Meanwhile, melt 2 tablespoons butter in pan and sauté onion. Wipe and slice mushrooms thickly; add to the pan and sprinkle with lemon juice. Cook gently until tender but not mushy. In another pan, make a roux: melt 2 tablespoons butter and mix in the flour. Pour in chicken stock and wine; cook, whisking constantly, until thickened. Season with salt, tarragon, and white pepper, and stir in cheese. Mix ¾ of the sauce with the rice, mushrooms, and shrimp. Reserve some shrimp for garnish. Butter a 2-quart casserole and spoon in mixture; arrange shrimp on top; spoon on additional sauce. Cover and bake at 350° for 20 minutes. Sprinkle with parsley.
Yield: 8–10 servings
Mrs. John Kris

BAKED BLUEFISH

3 pounds bluefish fillets
2 tablespoons mayonnaise
2 tablespoons sour cream
2 tablespoons Dijon mustard
2 tablespoons lemon juice
¼ teaspoon black pepper
½ teaspoon salt
chopped dill or parsley to taste (optional)

Preheat oven to 350°. Oil a rectangular baking dish. Arrange the bluefish fillets, skin down, in the baking dish. Combine remaining ingredients and spread evenly over the fish. For medium-thickness fillets, bake about 30 minutes. For very thick fillets, bake about 40 minutes. For added color, broil for the last 5 minutes.
Yield: 6–8 servings
Mrs. Juris Udris

SWORDFISH WITH WINE AND SOUR CREAM

2 pounds swordfish (allow ½ pound per person)
salt and pepper to taste
⅛ pound butter
2 teaspoons grated onion
½ cup white wine

SAUCE:
1 chicken bouillon cube
1 tablespoon sour cream
¼ cup white wine

Place the fish in a shallow baking dish. Season with salt and pepper. Spread butter over fish. Sprinkle with onion. Pour ½ cup wine over fish. Bake in 400° oven until tender (about 20–30 minutes), basting occasionally. Then brown the fish under the broiler. For the sauce, put bouillon cube, sour cream, and wine in a saucepan. Heat until bouillon cube is dissolved, stirring occasionally. Place fish on a warm platter and pour sauce over fish. Serve at once.
Yield: 4 servings
Mrs. Wayne K. Elliott

CONDIMENTS AND PRESERVES

SWEET AND SOUR MUSTARD SAUCE
Delicious with your holiday ham!

1 cup brown sugar, packed tight
⅓ cup dry mustard
1 teaspoon flour

½ cup water
½ cup cider vinegar
2 eggs, beaten

Mix dry ingredients together. Add liquids and eggs in a saucepan. Cook over slow heat, stir-

ring constantly with a whisk until thickened, about 15 minutes.
Yield: 2 cups
Mrs. George Sweeney

HUNTER'S SAUCE
Excellent with wild duck or cornish hens!

½ cup red currant jelly
¼ cup red port wine
¼ cup chili sauce or catsup
2 tablespoons butter
dash Worcestershire sauce

Melt ingredients together and serve.
Yield: 1 cup
Mrs. Winston R. Hindle, Jr.

SPICED WILD GRAPE CONSERVE
This recipe came to my mother from Mrs. Thomas Whitney Surrette, who lived in the large brick-end house diagonally across from the First Parish Church. Her husband, a famous musicologist, ran the Concord Summer School of Music. This is really a New England recipe; it goes compatibly with woodcock, duck, goose, or venison, but it is also good with roast beef or steak.

7 pounds wild grapes (they are very tart)
½ cup water
3½ pounds granulated sugar
1 cup cider vinegar
2 ounces whole cloves, together with
1 ounce stick cinnamon in cheesecloth bag

Separate grape skins from pulp. Boil skins in water in a pressure cooker for 20 to 30 minutes or boil *slowly* over burner for about 1½ hours, tightly covered. (Do not allow moisture to get too low; grapes burn easily.) Boil pulp and juice until soft. Strain. Add sugar, vinegar, spice bag, and skins. Boil to marmalade stage. Put into sterile jelly glasses. When cool and firm, cover with paraffin.
Yield: 12–16 jars
Mrs. Henry S. Drinker

ORANGE MARMALADE
This is my grandmother's recipe.

1 grapefruit
1 large orange
1 lemon
2 quarts water
5 pounds granulated sugar

Put the fruit through a meat chopper or food processor. Add the water and let stand overnight. In the morning, boil about 45 minutes and set away until the next day. Add the sugar and boil until jelly temperature on candy thermometer. Place in sterilized jelly jars and seal with paraffin wax.
Yield: 36 ounces
Mrs. George S. Reichenbach

CRANBERRY CHUTNEY

2 cups water
2 cups granulated sugar
2 tablespoons vinegar
2 tablespoons brown sugar
½ teaspoon salt
1 cup raisins
¼ teaspoon ginger
1 pound cranberries

Bring water and sugar to a boil and add remaining ingredients. Simmer, stirring occasionally, until berries pop. Put up as a preserve.
Yield: 6 cups
Mrs. Winston R. Hindle, Jr.

BRANDIED CRANBERRY SAUCE
This is an original recipe. It is extremely simple and very popular in our family.

1 quart fresh cranberries
1 cup water
1 cup granulated sugar
1 orange, well chopped
¼ cup brandy

Wash cranberries. Heat water and sugar to melt sugar. Add cranberries and chopped or-

ange and boil until cranberries pop. Remove from heat and add brandy. Cool and refrigerate. Will last indefinitely in glass containers in the refrigerator.
Yield: 1 quart
Can be frozen
Mrs. Ralph Livingston

MINCEMEAT
This is a wonderful recipe for mincemeat given to me by an 80-year-old woman who got it from her grandmother. It works well with any kind of meat but was meant for venison.

1 cup chopped venison (or beef or pork)
2 cups chopped apple
½ cup chopped suet
1⅓ cups granulated sugar
1 cup cider
½ cup syrup from sweet pickle jar
¼ pound citron, chopped
⅔ cup raisins (Sultana preferred)
⅔ cup currants
1 teaspoon salt
1 teaspoon mace
¼ teaspoon ground cloves
½ teaspoon ground cinnamon
gratings of nutmeg

Mix all the ingredients and cook 1 hour. Place into sterilized jars. Each quart is enough for one pie.

This mincemeat can also be used as a condiment for peaches. Fill centers of peaches with mincemeat and bake in buttered pan for 20 minutes at 350°. Serve hot with meat or salad.
Yield: about 6 quarts
Mrs. Joyce Webster (mincemeat)
Mrs. Charles W. Chamberlain (peach variations)

GRANDMA CROSBY'S BREAD AND BUTTER PICKLES
I inherited this recipe from my husband's Grandmother Crosby, who originally came from Kentucky, and lived in the state of Washington all her married life.

25 to 30 medium-size unpeeled cucumbers
8 large white onions
2 large sweet peppers, 1 red and 1 green
1 cup salt (DO NOT use table salt. Get ½ pound ground pure salt)
5 cups cider vinegar
5 cups granulated sugar
2 tablespoons mustard seed
1 teaspoon turmeric
½ teaspoon whole cloves

Wash cucumbers and slice paper thin. Chop or thinly slice onions and peppers and combine with cucumbers and salt. Let stand 3 hours. Drain (squeeze out as much liquid as possible). Combine vinegar, sugar, and spices in large kettle and bring to a boil. Pack while hot into sterilized jars. Seal at once.
Yield: Approximately 3 quarts
Mrs. J. Raymond Young

WATERMELON PICKLES
These are the best watermelon pickles I have ever tasted. Every summer my mother-in-law, Mrs. C. J. Jacoby, used to make a batch that would barely last through the year and was always a welcome gift.

watermelon rind
7 cups granulated sugar
1 pint white vinegar
½ teaspoon oil of cinnamon
½ teaspoon oil of cloves

Select a watermelon with a thick rind. Trim off the green skin and pink flesh and cut into size to fit into your jars, or into 1-inch cubes. There should be enough for 2½ quarts. Place rind in large saucepan and cover with boiling water. Boil until rind can be pierced easily with a fork, about 10 minutes. Drain well. In another saucepan, combine sugar, vinegar, oil of cloves, and oil of cinnamon. Bring to a boil. Pour over rind. Let stand overnight at room temperature. For the next three mornings, bring to the boiling point and let stand overnight. On the fourth morning, again heat to the boiling point. Turn at once into hot, sterilized pint preserve jars. Seal.
Yield: 4–6 pints
Mrs. Dean L. Jacoby

VEGETABLES AND SALADS

BAKED BEANS

I have shared this recipe with many of my Concord friends. It is so good you will have an empty pot.

1 pound pea beans, yellow eyed beans, or kidney beans
1 teaspoon baking soda
½ cup granulated sugar
3 tablespoons molasses
1 tablespoon maple syrup
¾ teaspoon ginger
1 teaspoon dry mustard
¼ teaspoon pepper
2 teaspoons salt
¼ teaspoon parsley flakes
1 tablespoon catsup
⅛ pound butter or margarine
¼ teaspoon thyme

Pick beans over carefully; wash and soak overnight. In the morning, throw the water away and parboil beans in fresh water. When the water comes to a boil, add the soda (to remove the snappers). Do not overdo. Rinse thoroughly. Put into a bean pot and add rest of ingredients. Add enough hot water to cover beans. Bake 5 to 6 hours at 275°. Off and on during the day, add a little hot water.
Yield: 8 servings
Mrs. J. Raymond Young

MARINATED GREEN BEAN SALAD

1½ pounds fresh green beans
salt to taste
Red Wine Vinaigrette Dressing (see p. 71)
1 pint cherry tomatoes, stemmed, washed, and dried
lettuce leaves
chopped parsley
2 hard-cooked eggs, minced

Prepare beans by boiling in salted water until just crisp and tender (about 6 minutes). Drain and refresh with cold water. Dry beans, then toss in a bowl with dressing to coat. Marinate at least 1 hour. Marinate tomatoes in a separate bowl. Arrange lettuce leaves in a shallow bowl or platter. Place beans on top and tomatoes around the edges. Garnish in the middle with eggs and chopped parsley.
Yield: 6 servings
Mrs. John Kris

HARVARD BEETS

At Christmas our family traditionally has rib roast of beef with Yorkshire pudding; Harvard beets; a lettuce, green bean, asparagus, and pimiento salad shaped to resemble a wreath; and sweet potato pie for dessert.

¼ cup vinegar
½ cup granulated sugar
2 teaspoons cornstarch
large piece butter
pinch salt (optional)
2 cans beets, well drained

In top of double boiler, combine vinegar, sugar, and cornstarch. Cook over *direct* heat, stirring constantly until mixture is clear (about 5 minutes). Place over hot water, add beets, and butter. Heat thoroughly.
Yield: 4 plentiful servings
Mrs. William H. Butler

SWEET POTATOES IN ORANGE CUPS

8 oranges
34 ounces cooked sweet potatoes
½ cup orange juice
3 tablespoons butter at room temperature
3 tablespoons dark brown sugar
¼ teaspoon ground nutmeg
¼ teaspoon ground cloves
salt and pepper to taste
paprika

Squeeze oranges; save juice and orange cups. Put orange cups in large buttered baking dish. Combine in a bowl, using a mixer, the sweet

potatoes, orange juice, butter, brown sugar, nutmeg, cloves, salt, and pepper. Mix until smooth. Fill the orange cups with sweet-potato mixture. Can be frozen at this point or bake in a 350° oven, uncovered, for 20 to 30 minutes. Sprinkle with paprika before baking.
Yield: 16 servings
Can be frozen
Mrs. George Sweeney, Jr.

BAKED ACORN SQUASH WITH SAUSAGE
This recipe would be part of the menu for a big Colonial Thanksgiving dinner.

4 acorn squash
12 links pork sausage
4 tablespoons melted butter
8 tablespoons honey
salt

Preheat oven to 350°. Cut each squash in half and scoop out the seeds. Put squash in a shallow pan, cut side down. Put in oven and bake for 35 minutes. While squash are baking, cook sausages in a skillet until they are browned. Remove squash from oven, turn them over, brush the insides with melted butter, and sprinkle them lightly with salt. Drizzle a tablespoon of honey over the inside of each half and put 3 brown sausage links in each. Bake at 350° for 25 minutes longer.
Yield: 8 squash halves
Miss Grace E. Gordon

TOMATO MUSHROOM CASSEROLE
This is a delightful discovery I invented from leftovers. It is hearty and good as both a side dish and a meatless main meal.

1 pound fresh mushrooms
1½ cups butter or margarine
3 1-pound cans stewed tomatoes, drained and juice reserved
6 tablespoons flour
2 cups juice from tomatoes
1 tablespoon finely chopped onion
2 tablespoons chopped chives
¼ teaspoon salt
1¼ cups seasoned bread crumbs

¼ cup Parmesan cheese, grated
¼ teaspoon oregano
garlic salt to taste
onion salt to taste

Slice mushrooms thickly and brown in 6 tablespoons butter for about 10 minutes. Put half the tomatoes in a large casserole, followed by half the mushrooms; repeat. In the same pan you cooked the mushrooms, make a cream sauce by melting 6 tablespoons of butter, stirring in the flour and, when thick, adding 2 cups reserved juice from tomatoes (add tomato juice or water if not enough); stir over low heat until thick, then add onion, chives, and salt. Pour over tomatoes and mushrooms. Poke to get sauce to bottom. Melt ¾ cup of butter, add rest of ingredients, and spread on top. Bake at 350° for 30 minutes or until brown and bubbling.
Yield: 10–15 servings
Can be frozen
Mrs. Thomas G. Doig

PORTSMOUTH SALAD
This salad was concocted by my father, Edward V. Papin, for a group of friends in a small restaurant specializing in broiled lobster in Portsmouth, New Hampshire (hence the name). He never measured any of the ingredients, yet it always turned out the same.

1 clove garlic
3 hard-cooked eggs
¼ pound Roquefort cheese
1 flat dessertspoon salt
½ flat dessertspoon dry mustard
¾ flat teaspoon black pepper
¾ flat teaspoon paprika
3 tablespoons Worcestershire sauce
½ cup cream
4 tablespoons tarragon vinegar
3 tablespoons olive oil
3 heads lettuce
3 sliced boiled potatoes

Crush the garlic in a large bowl with a little cream, then discard the garlic. Add all solid ingredients except the egg whites, lettuce, and potatoes. Pour Worcestershire and a little cream over the mass and work to a smooth

paste. Add remaining cream gradually, stirring until all is smooth; then add the vinegar and finally the oil, beating vigorously, to make the dressing light and foamy. Finally add the minced egg whites, lettuce, and potatoes and mix thoroughly. Correct the seasoning if desired.
Yield: 12 servings
Mrs. Frederic Gooding

RED WINE VINAIGRETTE DRESSING

1 teaspoon salt
½ teaspoon freshly ground black pepper
1 clove garlic, minced
1 shallot, minced
3 teaspoons Dijon-style mustard
¼ cup red wine vinegar
2 or 3 tablespoons lemon juice
½ cup olive oil mixed with ½ cup vegetable oil

In a bowl (or a processor with steel blade) whisk salt, pepper, garlic, shallot, mustard, vinegar, and lemon juice until frothy. Gradually add the oil, whisking all the while. The dressing should be quite frothy. Refrigerate if not using immediately. Let dressing warm to room temperature and whisk again before using.
Yield: 6 servings
Mrs. John Kris

BREADS

CHRISTMAS IRISH BREAD

2 cups sifted flour
3 teaspoons baking powder
½ teaspoon salt
¼ cup sugar
¼ cup butter
⅓ cup raisins
1 egg, beaten
⅔ cup milk (approximately)

Combine dry ingredients. Sift them. Work in butter (cut into pieces) until mixture resembles very small peas. In another bowl, beat egg into milk. Add raisins to flour mixture. Pour milk mixture into flour mixture and stir until batter comes away from the sides of the bowl. Put out on a lightly floured board and shape into a round loaf. Bake in a buttered 8- or 9-inch round pan at 400° for about 30 minutes. (Top will be golden and a toothpick inserted will come out dry.)

FROSTING:
1 cup confectioners' sugar
milk, a few drops
vanilla, a few drops

Mix above ingredients. Pour over top of bread and top with a cherry.
Yield: 1 loaf
Mrs. Louis K. McNally, Jr.

BROWN BREAD

1 cup rye flour
1 cup cornmeal
1 cup graham flour
1 teaspoon baking soda
1½ teaspoons salt
1 cup molasses
2 cups light cream

Sift together flour, cornmeal, and soda. Add salt, molasses, and cream and make a batter. Put batter in two buttered 1-quart pudding molds (or three buttered 1-pound coffee tins— but only fill them ¾ full). Secure tops of pudding molds. Place in boiling water to reach ⅓ of the way up mold (or coffee can) and steam for 3 hours. Serve with butter.
Yield: 2 1-quart loaves or 3 1-pound-coffee-can loaves
Can be frozen
Mrs. L. K. DeLamarter

APPLESAUCE RAISIN BREAD

I make this at Christmastime for our friends and neighbors. Added fun is that it makes the house smell heavenly!

1 egg, slightly beaten
1 cup applesauce
½ cup melted butter
½ cup granulated sugar
¼ cup brown sugar, packed
2 cups unsifted all-purpose flour
2 teaspoons baking powder
¾ teaspoon salt
½ teaspoon soda
½ teaspoon cinnamon
1 teaspoon nutmeg
½ cup seedless raisins (I mix white and dark)
1 cup coarsely chopped pecans or walnuts
powdered sugar

Combine the egg, applesauce, butter, granulated and brown sugars, blending well. Stir in flour, baking powder, salt, soda, cinnamon, and nutmeg. Stir until smooth. Stir in raisins and chopped nuts. Turn batter into a well-greased 5 x 9-inch loaf pan or fluted mold with tube that holds about 1 quart. Bake at 350° for 1 hour or a little longer. Dust with powdered sugar when cool.
Yield: 1 large loaf
Mrs. John Kris

CRACKER ROUNDS

Use with soups, as bread, or for appetizers.

2 cups flour
¼ teaspoon salt
4 tablespoons butter
¾ cup cold water
melted butter

Mix together all ingredients except melted butter. Roll out half of the mixture at a time, *very thinly*, as evenly as possible. Place on a greased cookie pan in a preheated 500° oven. When brown, brush over with melted butter. Put under the broiler for a few seconds. These can be broken into pieces or the dough can be gone over with a pie crimper before baking to make them more uniform. They can be kept in a covered container and warmed before using.
Yield: 3 or 4 dozen, according to the size they are broken into
Mrs. Rosealie Frost

DESSERTS AND SWEETS

APRICOT MOUSSE

1 1-pound-14-ounce can whole apricots, drained (save liquid)
1 3-ounce package lemon gelatin
1 teaspoon vanilla
3 tablespoons apricot brandy
1 cup heavy cream, whipped
1 package lady fingers

Set aside 2 whole apricots for decoration. Purée rest of drained and pitted apricots in blender. Heat reserved apricot liquid plus enough water to measure 1¾ cups to the boiling point. Remove from heat and add gelatin; stir until dissolved. Add puréed apricots, vanilla, and brandy, then chill until mixture begins to thicken. Whip cream. Beat apricot mixture slightly and fold into whipped cream. Line a crystal bowl with lady fingers and pour in mousse. Refrigerate at least 4 hours (overnight is best). Decorate with reserved apricots and additional whipped cream.
Yield: 6 servings
Mrs. Peter Kondon

SUPRÊME AU CHOCOLAT GÂTEAU

A chocolate mousse between layers of chocolate meringue—quite fantastic! One of the treats the parents from Brooks School, Concord, look forward to at the parents' evening.

MERINGUE:
5 egg whites
pinch of cream of tartar
¾ cup granulated sugar
1¾ cups confectioners' sugar
⅓ cup unsweetened cocoa

Beat egg whites with pinch of cream of tartar to a soft peak. Beat in granulated sugar a little at a time until it holds a firm peak. Sift confectioners' sugar and cocoa in and fold in carefully. Cover three baking sheets with waxed paper and divide meringue into three squares or circles of even depth. Bake in oven at 300° for 1 hour and 15 minutes. Remove from tray while still warm.

MOUSSE:
12 ounces semisweet chocolate
1 ounce baking chocolate
7 egg whites
¼ teaspoon cream of tartar
3 cups heavy cream, chilled
1½ teaspoons vanilla
finely grated orange peel (optional)

Melt semisweet and baking chocolate in top of double boiler. Allow to cool until lukewarm. (If wanted, add peel from one orange finely grated.) Beat egg whites with cream of tartar until firm. In a separate bowl, beat heavy cream with vanilla until firm. Gently fold chocolate and egg whites, then fold in cream.

Place first layer of meringue on your serving plate and, using nearly ⅓ of the mousse, cover with a thick layer. Place second layer of meringue on top and cover with a thick layer of mousse. Finally, add the last layer of meringue and cover top and sides with remaining mousse. Sprinkle a little grated chocolate on top for decoration. Refrigerate. May be made the day before if kept covered in the refrigerator.
Yield: 8–10 servings
Mrs. Seymour A. DiMare

CRANBERRY SHERBET
This is my mother-in-law's (Mrs. C. J. Jacoby) recipe. She always makes it at Thanksgiving and Christmas. Although we eat it with din-

ner in place of cranberry sauce, it could also serve as a light dessert.

2 cups fresh cranberries
2½ cups water
1 teaspoon unflavored gelatin
2 cups granulated sugar
2 lemons
2 egg whites, beaten until stiff

Cook the cranberries in the water, covered, until the skins pop open. Force through a sieve. Add gelatin while cranberries are still warm and stir well. Add sugar and the grated rind and juice of the lemons. Turn into ice-cube trays and freeze until firm. Turn into chilled bowl. With mixer, beat until thick and mushy. Add the beaten egg whites. Refreeze. Whip once more and refreeze.
Yield: approximately 1 quart
Mrs. Dean L. Jacoby

LEMON CREAM
Fun to make and delicious!

juice of 3 lemons
⅔ cup granulated sugar
1 pint heavy cream

In a deep bowl, stir lemon juice and sugar together until sugar is dissolved. Put bowl on floor. Stand AS HIGH AS POSSIBLE and pour heavy cream from this height in a steady stream into the bowl. Cream will whip itself (the higher you stand the more froth there will be). Cover and chill several hours or overnight. This will be quite liquid when served, but has a wonderfully refreshing taste.
Yield: 6 servings
Mrs. Jonathan Keyes

INDIAN PUDDING
This is a family recipe my grandmother served at least as long ago as the turn of the century.

6 cups milk
½ cup butter
½ cup yellow cornmeal

¼ cup flour
1 teaspoon salt
½ cup molasses
3 eggs, beaten
1 cup granulated sugar
1 teaspoon cinnamon
1 teaspoon nutmeg
1 cup seedless raisins
heavy cream, whipped
sugar to taste
vanilla to taste

Scald milk and butter in top of large double boiler. Mix cornmeal, flour, and salt; stir in the molasses. Thin the mixture with about ½ cup of scalded milk, then gradually add the mixture to the scalded milk in double boiler. Cook, stirring, until thickened. Pour over other ingredients mixed together in a casserole—eggs, sugar, and spices. Stir until smooth. Stir in the raisins and bake 2 hours in a 250° oven. The pudding must cool about an hour to be at its best. It should be reheated to warm temperature if it has been chilled. It should be served with whipped cream which has been only slightly sweetened, if at all, and flavored with vanilla.
Yield: 8–10 servings
Mrs. Jay W. Forrester

PUMPKIN PUDDING
Better than pumpkin pie!

4 cups pumpkin
2 cups brown sugar
1 cup granulated sugar
2 tablespoons molasses
3 teaspoons cinnamon
3 teaspoons ginger
dash nutmeg
1½ teaspoons salt
2 tablespoons melted butter
2 tablespoons brandy
6 eggs, beaten
4 cups heavy cream, whipped

Mix pumpkin with only 1 cup brown sugar and rest of ingredients. Butter 2 small casseroles or 1 large one. Spread the other cup of brown sugar on the bottom. Pour in mixture. Place in

a pan of boiling water. Bake at 350° for 50 minutes or longer, until set. Chill. Cover the top with sweetened whipped cream or with ice cream.
Yield: 10–12 servings
Can be frozen
Mrs. Pierce B. Browne

OLD BALTIMORE WINE JELLY
It has been a favorite dessert for many years in Baltimore, and my Concord friends seem to like it!

1 cup water
1 lemon
1 envelope gelatin
salt
½ cup granulated sugar
1½ cups sherry

Grate the rind of the lemon and boil it for 5 minutes in the water. Squeeze the juice of the lemon and mix it with the gelatin to soften. Then add the boiling water and lemon rind. Stir until dissolved and add a pinch of salt, sugar, and sherry. Mold. Serve with whipped or plain cream.
Yield: 4 small custard-size molds
Mrs. Newell Garfield

PERFECT PIE CRUST

1 pound lard or 1 cup margarine and ½ cup
  shortening
4 cups flour, presifted
1 tablespoon granulated sugar
1½ teaspoons salt
1 egg, beaten
1 tablespoon white vinegar
½ cup cold water

In a large bowl, cut shortening into flour. Add remaining ingredients. Cut these in well. Finally, with your hands, really work pastry until it has a nice moist consistency. Refrigerate 1 hour, if you wish, for easier rolling.
Yield: crust for 3 small or 2 large pies
Mrs. Gilbert K. Gailius

CRANBERRY PIE

We have no idea how far back this recipe may go in its origin. We have never seen the recipe published, and it does not seem to be well known among old Cape Codders. My husband's 98-year-old mother was born on a New Hampshire farm that had its own cranberry bog. The homestead itself was so old that it had trap doors inside the front and back doors in case of Indian attacks.

2 cups chopped cranberries
1 cup granulated sugar
½ cup water
2 tablespoons molasses
2 tablespoons cornstarch

Mix all ingredients and cook in saucepan until thick and bubbly. Pour into 7-inch uncooked pie shell. For top crust, cut ¼-inch pastry strips and make a lattice top. Bake 10 minutes at 450°, then 20 minutes longer at 350°.
Yield: 1 pie
Mrs. Frederick W. Mears

LEMON SPONGE PIE

This recipe has been handed down in our family for five generations.

2 tablespoons flour
1 cup granulated sugar
pinch salt
juice of 1 large lemon
2 tablespoons melted butter
2 eggs, separated
1 cup milk
1 unbaked pie shell

Mix flour, sugar, and salt. Add lemon juice, melted butter, and beaten egg yolks. Blend well. Add milk. Fold in stiffly beaten egg whites until well blended with mixture. Pour into unbaked pie shell. Bake at 350° for 35 minutes or until golden brown.
Yield: 1 pie
Mrs. Frederick S. Jones, II

FROZEN PUMPKIN PIE

1 10-inch or 2 8-inch baked pie shells
1 pint vanilla ice cream, softened
2 cups cooked pumpkin
1 cup granulated sugar
½ teaspoon salt
½ teaspoon ginger
¼ teaspoon cloves
1½ cups whipping cream
1 cup slivered almonds
¼ cup granulated sugar

Spread ice cream in shell and freeze. Mix pumpkin with 1 cup sugar and spices. Beat 1 cup cream until stiff and fold into pumpkin mixture. Spread over ice cream. Freeze at least 4 hours. Place almonds and ¼ cup sugar in pan over low heat. When sugar begins to caramelize, stir constantly until golden brown. Cool on buttered cookie sheet and break apart. To serve, allow pie to soften somewhat, garnish with remaining cream, whipped, and top with almonds.
Yield: 1 10-inch or 2 8-inch pies
Can be frozen
Mrs. Henry S. Thompson, Jr.

WILD BLACKBERRY TURNOVERS

This recipe was developed at the Hawthorne Inn, Concord, Mass.

DOUGH:
¼ cup honey or ½ cup granulated sugar
½ cup butter
2 eggs
1 teaspoon vanilla
2½ cups Cornell Mix
2 teaspoons baking powder
½ teaspoon salt

CORNELL MIX:
1 tablespoon soy flour
1 tablespoon dry milk
1 tablespoon bran
1 tablespoon rye flour
1 teaspoon wheat germ
plus enough unbleached white flour for mix
*   to equal 1 cup*

Cream honey or sugar and butter; beat eggs well into mixture until light. Add vanilla. Sift or mix well Cornell Mix, baking powder, and salt; add to butter mixture. Blend until smooth; chill. Preheat oven to 400°. While dough is chilling, make filling.

FILLING:
1 quart fresh (or frozen) blackberries
2 tablespoons melted butter
1 teaspoon cinnamon sweetened with sugar
*   to taste (granulated or brown sugar may*
*   be used)*
1 tablespoon flour, for thickening
less than ¼ teaspoon nutmeg or lemon juice
*   (optional)*

Combine ingredients and mix well. When dough is stiff enough to be handled, turn out portion onto floured board. Roll out to ¼-inch thick and cut into 1½ dozen 4-inch circles. Place a heaping tablespoon of blackberry mixture on front half of circle of dough; fold back half over to form top. Pinch edge firmly; prick top with fork. Dust lightly with sugar and cinnamon. Place on lightly greased cookie sheet and bake in preheated oven until golden, about 15 minutes.
Yield: 1½ dozen turnovers
Hawthorne Inn

BLUEBERRY GRUNT

12 ounces frozen blueberries, thawed
½ cup granulated sugar
2 cups sifted flour
1 tablespoon baking powder
¼ teaspoon salt
2 tablespoons butter or margarine
¾ cup milk (approximately)
grated rind of 1 orange

Mix blueberries with sugar and pour mixture into heavily greased 1½-quart mold. (If berries are packed with sugar syrup, pour berries with syrup into greased mold and omit the sugar.) Sift together flour, baking powder, and salt. Cut in butter or margarine until particles are fine. Stir in enough milk to make a soft dough, about the consistency of a drop biscuit dough.

Spoon dough over berries. Cover mold tightly with lid or with a piece of greased foil. Place mold in a deep kettle and fill with boiling water halfway up the side of the mold. Cover kettle and simmer 1½ hours. Remove mold from kettle, uncover, loosen edge with sharp knife, and invert mold on serving plate while still hot. Allow syrup in the bottom of the mold to run down pudding into platter. Accompany with Fluffy Nutmeg Sauce (see p. 81).
Yield: 1½ quarts
Mrs. Paul R. Dinsmore

CONCORD GRAPE JAM SQUARES

½ cup shortening
½ cup granulated sugar
1 egg
½ teaspoon lemon rind
1½ cups flour
1½ teaspoons baking powder
½ teaspoon salt
½ teaspoon cinnamon
¼ teaspoon ground cloves
4 tablespoons milk
¾ cup grape jam

Cream shortening and sugar until light and fluffy. Add well-beaten egg and lemon rind. Mix well. Sift together flour, baking powder, salt, cinnamon, and cloves. Stir milk into mixture and add the sifted dry ingredients. Spread half of the batter in a greased 9 x 9 x 2-inch pan, then spread jam over the batter. Add the rest of the batter over that. Bake at 400° for 25 minutes. When cool, cut into squares. Can be made with other preserves: orange, peach, apricot, blueberry, etc.
Yield: 20 squares
Can be frozen
Mrs. Alva Morrison

FRUITCAKE

2 cups butter
2 cups granulated sugar
10 eggs
½ cup grape juice
½ cup dark molasses

4 cups cake flour
1¾ teaspoons baking powder
2 teaspoons mace
1 teaspoon nutmeg
¾ teaspoon salt
1 teaspoon ginger
1½ teaspoons ground cloves
2 pounds raisins
2 pounds currants
2 pounds candied orange peel, chopped
½ pound citron, shredded
¼ pound candied cherries, chopped
¼ pound candied pineapple, chopped

Cream together butter and sugar until well blended. Add eggs one at a time, beating well after each addition. Stir in grape juice and molasses. Sift together all dry ingredients and mix thoroughly with fruit. Add to batter and mix well. Pack batter into cake tins that have been greased and lined with waxed paper or brown paper, also greased. Bake in a very slow oven, 250°, with a shallow pan of water on a lower shelf, for about 3 hours or until a cake tester comes out clean. Remove from pans, peel off paper, cool, wrap well, and store for at least 30 days. Moisten occasionally with rum.

To decorate for Christmas: Reduce marzipan to spreading consistency by adding brandy or rum drop by drop, and cover cake completely with a thin layer. Allow to set, then ice with a meringue frosting and decorate with holiday motifs in green and red frostings.
Yield: 5 2-pound cakes
Mrs. F. Harrie Richardson

ANGEL GINGERBREAD

½ cup granulated sugar
¼ cup butter
1 cup flour
1 teaspoon baking soda
1 teaspoon cinnamon
1 teaspoon ginger
½ teaspoon salt
1 egg, slightly beaten
¼ cup molasses
½ cup regular strength coffee or hot water

Cream together sugar and butter. Sift flour with other dry ingredients and add to the sugar/butter mixture. Blend well. Add the slightly beaten egg. Mix and add the molasses. Add the coffee or hot water last. Bake in an 8-inch-square greased pan in 350° oven for 25 minutes. Serve with a dollop of whipped cream or applesauce.
Yield: 1 8-inch-square cake
Miss Dorothy I. Malone

ORANGE-DATE CAKE
This is a cake my aunt prepared for our family Christmas for many, many years.

1 cup butter or shortening
2 cups granulated sugar
4 eggs
1⅓ cups buttermilk
1 teaspoon soda, mixed into the buttermilk
4 cups flour
1 cup chopped pecans
1 8-ounce package dates, chopped
2 tablespoons grated orange rind

ORANGE GLAZE:
2 cups granulated sugar
1 cup fresh or frozen orange juice
2 tablespoons grated orange rind

Cream butter and sugar thoroughly. Add eggs one at a time, beating well after each addition. Add flour alternately with buttermilk/soda. Fold in pecans, dates, and orange rind. Bake in greased, floured 10-inch tube or bundt pan. Bake 1½ hours in a slow oven (275° to 300°). Coat while hot with orange glaze.

To make glaze: Combine ingredients in a saucepan and dissolve—don't boil. Poke holes in cake with toothpick or fork and pour or spoon glaze over cake.
Yield: 1 cake
Mrs. Joe B. Wyatt

SIMPLE POUND CAKE WITH APRICOT BRANDY GLAZE
This cake is good served with vanilla ice cream with glaze, strawberries, pineapple, or

chocolate sauce over the ice cream. Also perfectly good plain.

3¾ cups confectioners' sugar
1½ cups margarine, softened
3 large eggs, room temperature
1 teaspoon real vanilla extract
1 teaspoon lemon extract
3¾ cups sifted flour
1 teaspoon baking powder
1 teaspoon mace
1 cup milk, room temperature
⅔ cup apricot jam
¼ cup apricot brandy

Cream sugar and margarine until fluffy, beat in eggs one at a time, add vanilla and lemon, add ⅓ of the flour, baking powder, and mace sifted together, followed each time by ⅓ of the milk. Mix until smooth and pour into greased 10-inch tube pan; bake at 325° for about 1 hour (test with toothpick). Let cool in pan about 15 minutes; turn out carefully. Turn right side up and glaze with apricot jam that has been mashed smooth and heated with apricot brandy.
Yield: 1 cake
Mrs. John Benjamin

PINEAPPLE UPSIDE DOWN CAKE

½ cup brown sugar
⅛ pound butter
2 tablespoons pineapple juice
pineapple slices
maraschino cherries
4 eggs
1 cup granulated sugar
¾ teaspoon almond flavoring
5 tablespoons milk
1 cup flour
¾ teaspoon baking powder

Melt together brown sugar, butter, and pineapple juice. Arrange pineapple slices with maraschino cherry in center of each in the bottom of an old-fashioned cast-iron skillet and add melted brown sugar, butter, and pineapple juice mixture. Separate eggs. Beat whites until stiff and set aside. Beat yolks until creamy,

then add granulated sugar. Add almond flavoring and milk. Beat in flour and baking powder. Fold in egg whites, mix, and pour over the pineapple slices, etc., in skillet. Bake 30 to 35 minutes at 350°. When cooled somewhat, turn skillet upside down onto cake plate for easy removal. Serve hot with whipped cream.
Yield: 1 cake
Mrs. Richard Young

OLDE ENGLISH SEED CAKE

3 cups sifted all-purpose flour
1 cup granulated sugar
½ teaspoon salt
2 teaspoons baking powder
1 cup butter or margarine
3 eggs, well beaten
1⅔ cups evaporated milk
1 tablespoon caraway seeds
⅓ cup finely chopped candied orange peel

Sift together into large mixing bowl the flour, sugar, salt, and baking powder. Cut in the butter or margarine with pastry blender or fork until mixture resembles cornmeal. Add eggs, evaporated milk, caraway seeds, and candied peel. Beat just until smooth. Turn into a well-greased 10-inch tube pan. Bake in a moderate oven (350°) until done when tested, about 1 hour. Cool in pan 10 minutes. Remove and cool completely on rack. May be prepared ahead and stored for richer flavor.
Yield: 1 cake
Mrs. Paul R. Dinsmore

ENGLISH TRIFLE
This recipe was given to my mother, Bertha W. Joslin, in 1917 by an English war bride who was preparing it for her baby's christening.

1 pound cake or
  1 16-ounce package lady fingers
½ cup sherry
20 ounces crushed pineapple
slivered almonds
1 pint heavy cream, whipped
red and green candied cherries, chopped

Line bottom and sides of a deep glass bowl, 8–10 inches in diameter, with slices of pound cake or lady fingers, moistened with the sherry, and let stand 30 minutes. Add the pineapple and let stand 4 hours. Top with the whipped cream, mounded in the center, and garnish with the almonds and the chopped cherries.
Yield: 8 servings
Mrs. Edgar W. Tucker

ANISE CAKES
These are the traditional family cookie for Christmas and Easter. I make at least a half dozen batches between Thanksgiving and Christmas. Neighborhood children say it means "Christmas is coming!"

4 large eggs
2 cups granulated sugar
1 teaspoon anise oil
4 cups flour
2 teaspoons baking powder
confectioners' sugar

Beat eggs with mixer, add sugar, and continue beating until sugar is dissolved. Add anise oil. Slowly add 2 cups flour, then add 1 cup flour sifted with 2 teaspoons baking powder. By hand, cut in last cup of flour. Put in refrigerator and chill at least 4 hours. Mixture may be frozen at this point. Dust rolling pin and area with confectioners' sugar. Take cold dough and roll (sprinkled with confectioners' sugar) ¼ inch thick. Again dust with a fine coat of confectioners' sugar to prevent sticking and press with Springerle board or rolling pin. Cut into blocks and place on ungreased cookie sheet. Put in cool area to "dry" for 6 to 8 hours or overnight. Bake at 375° for 10 to 15 minutes, until pale yellow. Remove to racks to cool.
Yield: 5 dozen cakes
Mrs. Richard Armknecht

GRANDMA'S CARROT COOKIES
These are great for leftover carrots, and they taste even better after "aging" a couple of days in a tin cookie box.

COOKIES:
1 cup shortening (can use ½ butter and ½ shortening)
¾ cup granulated sugar
1 cup cooked, mashed carrots (about 5 medium)
2 cups flour
2 teaspoons baking powder
1 teaspoon salt
1½ teaspoons vanilla

FROSTING:
2 tablespoons orange or lemon juice
grated rind of 1 lemon or orange
3 tablespoons butter
powdered sugar

Cream shortening and sugar; add remaining ingredients and mix well. Drop by teaspoonfuls and flatten to 2-inch diameter. Bake 20 minutes on ungreased sheets at 350°. Cool on rack. Frost.

To make frosting, combine juice, rind, and softened butter. Add powdered sugar to reach desired consistency.
Yield: 3 dozen cookies
Mrs. Joyce Webster

CHOCOLATE DROP COOKIES

COOKIES:
1 cup light brown sugar
½ cup butter
3 heaping tablespoons Dutch cocoa
1 egg
½ cup milk
1 teaspoon vanilla
1½ cups flour
2 teaspoons baking powder
1 cup chopped nuts

FROSTING:
4 tablespoons butter
3 heaping tablespoons Dutch cocoa
1½ cups powdered sugar
hot water

Melt sugar, butter, and cocoa in saucepan. Beat egg; add milk and vanilla. Stir in flour sifted with baking powder. Add to first mixture and add chopped nuts. If desired, omit nuts and sprinkle them on top of cookies after they are frosted. Drop from spoon onto greased cookie sheet, and bake about 15 minutes at 275°.

To make frosting: Melt butter and cocoa together, then add sugar and enough hot water to spread.
Yield: 4 dozen cookies
Mrs. David Reece

CHRISTMAS HEIRLOOM COOKIES
This is my mother's recipe.

COOKIES:
1 cup butter
1 tablespoon vanilla
1 cup confectioners' sugar
½ teaspoon salt
1¼ cups almonds, finely ground
2 cups flour, sifted

DECORATION:
½ cup confectioners' sugar
2 teaspoons cinnamon

Cream butter, vanilla, 1 cup confectioners' sugar, salt. Add almonds. Blend in flour. Shape dough into balls or crescents, using a rounded teaspoonful for each. Bake at 325° for 15 to 18 minutes. (Cookies will *not* be brown when done.) Roll cookies in the cinnamon and confectioners' sugar mixture while warm.
Yield: 4½ dozen cookies
Can be frozen
Mrs. Richard Spaulding

FILLED COOKIES
My mother liked this recipe.

COOKIES:
1 cup granulated sugar
½ cup shortening
1 egg
½ cup milk
2½ cups flour
2 teaspoons cream of tartar
1 teaspoon soda
1 teaspoon vanilla

FILLING:
1 cup chopped raisins
½ cup granulated sugar
½ cup water
1 teaspoon flour
2 or 3 slices lemon

Cream shortening and sugar; add other ingredients. Roll thin. Cut the roll, put cookies on pan, then put a teaspoon of filling on each. To make filling, cook all ingredients until thick. Place another cookie on top of each filled cookie, gently pressing the two edges together. Bake at 325° for 12 minutes or until delicately brown.
Yield: 2½ dozen cookies
Miss Faith Merrill Kimball

FRUITCAKE COOKIES

½ cup brown sugar
¼ cup butter
2 eggs, well beaten
1½ cups flour
1½ tablespoons milk
4 or 5 tablespoons whiskey
1½ teaspoons soda
½ teaspoon nutmeg
½ teaspoon cloves (ground)
½ teaspoon allspice
½ teaspoon cinnamon
1 teaspoon vanilla
½ pound pecan halves
½ to ¾ pound raisins
½ pound candied cherries
1 to 1½ pounds finely cut candied fruit

Cream butter and sugar together. Add eggs, flour, and milk alternately. Add whiskey, soda, spices, and vanilla. Last, add the nuts and candied fruit (*not* the cherries). Drop cookies on a greased cookie sheet. Top each cookie with half a cherry. Bake at 300° for 30 minutes.
Yield: 3–4 dozen cookies
Mrs. Todd Hixon

NUT COOKIES

½ cup butter
2 tablespoons granulated sugar
1 teaspoon vanilla
1 cup pecans
⅞ cup cake flour
powdered sugar

Cream butter and sugar together. Add vanilla. Add sifted flour and chopped pecans. Shape dough into small balls. Bake on greased cookie sheet in 300° oven for 30 minutes. Roll the cookies in powdered sugar when they come out of the oven.
Yield: 3 dozen cookies
Mrs. Richard H. Johnson

FLUFFY NUTMEG SAUCE

⅓ cup granulated sugar
1 tablespoon cornstarch
½ cup frozen orange juice concentrate, undiluted
½ cup water
2 tablespoons frozen lemon juice, undiluted
3 tablespoons butter or margarine
1 teaspoon ground nutmeg
1 cup heavy cream, whipped

Mix sugar with cornstarch. Gradually stir in orange juice concentrate, water, and lemon juice. Cook over low heat, stirring constantly, until mixture bubbles and thickens. Stir in butter or margarine and nutmeg. Cool. Fold in whipped cream and blend well. Chill until ready to serve. Stir again before serving.
Yield: about 2½ cups
Mrs. Paul Dinsmore

ALMOND PASTE
A paste for marzipan candies.

1½ cups whole blanched almonds
1½ cups sifted confectioners' sugar
1 egg white
1 teaspoon almond extract
¼ teaspoon salt
1½ teaspoons cornstarch

Grind the blanched almonds until fine. Add remaining ingredients. Work to a stiff paste. Refrigerate in airtight container. The longer this is refrigerated—even up to 1 month—the easier it will be to work.
Yield: 1⅓ cups paste
Mrs. Jonathan Keyes

SWEET SPICED PECANS

1 egg white
1 teaspoon water
½ cup granulated sugar
½ teaspoon salt
½ teaspoon cinnamon
Dash nutmeg
1 pound or 5 cups large pecans

Beat egg white with water until frothy. Combine sugar, salt, cinnamon, and nutmeg. Add slowly to egg white and beat to meringue consistency. Add pecans. Mix well to coat. Place in mound on buttered cookie sheet with sides. Bake in 225° oven for 1 hour. Stir every 15 minutes and spread out over entire surface of cookie sheet.
Yield: 5 cups nuts
Mrs. Wayne K. Elliott

SPUN SUGAR

2 cups granulated sugar
1 cup water
⅛ teaspoon cream of tartar

Dissolve sugar in water, bring slowly to boiling point, and boil to 280°. Add cream of tartar and continue boiling without stirring until the syrup reaches 310°. In the meantime, have ready 2 oiled wooden spoon handles securely anchored in kitchen-cabinet drawers, with a clean paper spread on the floor below. When the syrup reaches 310°, remove quickly to a pan of cold water to stop the boiling, then to a pan of hot water. Tint with food colors if desired. Dip the spinner (a spoon, large knife, or egg whip will serve) into the syrup and swing back and forth over the handles. The sugar falls in long threads. If syrup thickens as you work,

heat the water in the lower pan until the syrup melts and continue spinning. Use at once as decorative nests for ice cream, meringue glacé, baked Alaska, or Easter eggs.
Mrs. Adolphus Rumreich

APPLE FRITTERS

6 medium-size hard tart cooking apples
1 cup sugar
2 tablespoons cinnamon
2 cups all-purpose flour
2 cups beer
vegetable oil or shortening for deep frying
powdered sugar

Peel and core the apples, then slice into ½-inch-thick circles (hole in the middle). Mix the sugar with cinnamon and coat apple slices with it. Let stand in a cool place. In a large mixing bowl, sift flour; make a well in the middle and slowly pour the beer into it. With a hand beater, slowly mix the flour and beer until smooth. Be careful not to overmix; the batter should be slightly bubbly. Let stand until the deep-fry oil is hot. In a heavy saucepan or Dutch oven, heat the oil or shortening to 350°. The oil should be about 3 inches deep. Drop a few apple slices in the batter, coat them well, and drop them one by one in the hot oil. When the underside is golden brown, turn over. When both sides are brown, transfer with slotted spoon onto paper towels to drain off excess oil. Serve warm with a sprinkling of powdered sugar.
Yield: 20–25 fritters
Mrs. John Blinn

SPICED PEARS IN RED WINE
This is an excellent dessert for those times during the holidays when you've had your fill of really sweet dishes. It is perfect for a cold night, and can be made several days in advance!

6 pears, hard and unripe, preferably Bosc
2 cups granulated sugar
1 bottle dry red wine
6 to 8 cloves
1 2-inch-wide strip of orange peel, dried in a
  hot oven for about 10 minutes
1 stick of cinnamon

Peel pears carefully, trying to leave stems intact. Stand pears upright in an ovenproof casserole that has a tight-fitting cover. Pears should touch each other with no extra space. Add sugar. Pour in enough wine to half cover pears. Add cloves, orange peel, and cinnamon. Add enough water to cover the pears. Cover and bake at 175° until pears are tender when pierced. Time will vary with hardness of pears; approximately 6 hours. Chill. Serve with a bit of wine sauce. This keeps very well for 1 to 2 weeks.
Yield: 6 servings
Mrs. Gilbert P. Wozney

CANDIED FRUIT PEEL

Orange rind or grapefruit rind that has been
  soaked overnight in salt water
granulated sugar
water

Put rind in cold water, bring to a boil and boil for 10 minutes. Drain and repeat this process two more times. Drain and scrape away white part. Cut into strips. For each cup of rind, prepare a sugar syrup of 1 cup sugar to ⅓ cup water. Put rind in syrup and cook slowly until syrup is completely absorbed. Stir occasionally and watch carefully toward end of process. Cool the peel and coat the strips with granulated sugar. The sugared peel, when dry, may be dipped in melted semisweet chocolate.
Mrs. John Adams

BEVERAGES

SYLLABUB
This is an old recipe.

2 cups Madeira wine
5 tablespoons grated lemon rind
⅓ cup lemon juice
1 cup granulated sugar
3 cups milk
2 cups light cream
4 egg whites
½ cup sugar
nutmeg

Combine wine, lemon rind, and lemon juice. Add 1 cup of sugar and let mixture stand until sugar dissolves. Then add milk and cream and stir with rotary beater until frothy. Beat egg whites until stiff. Add ½ cup of sugar a little at a time, beating constantly until whites stand in peaks. Pour wine mixture into punch bowl. Top with puffs of egg white. Sprinkle with nutmeg.
Yield: 16 punch cups
Mrs. Floyd Verrill

CHRISTMAS BURGUNDY BOWL
This punch has been a holiday favorite for many years in my family.

46 ounces grapefruit juice
20 ounces frozen raspberries
¼ cup lemon juice
½ cup granulated sugar
⅛ teaspoon salt
3 large bottles sparkling Burgundy, well chilled

Combine all ingredients except wine and stir until sugar is dissolved and raspberries are slightly thawed. Pour into punch bowl over ice. When ready to serve, add wine and stir. Make sure a few raspberries get into each punch cup when pouring.
Yield: 40 regular-size punch cups
Mrs. Todd DeBinder

GUNNARSON GLÖGG
This is a powerful, warming drink suitable for any and all skål *rituals.*

1 quart water
1 cup white raisins
12 cardamoms, well crushed
12 whole cloves
1 orange rind, thinly peeled
2 sticks cinnamon
1 piece ginger root—3 or 4 slices, ⅛" thick, ½" wide, 2" long (all approximately)
1 gallon claret
½ gallon port
½ gallon brandy
½ gallon rum
1 quart aquavit
3–4 cups granulated sugar
½ cup almonds, blanched

Simmer all nonalcoholic items except almonds and sugar in a quart of water for 1 hour. Add alcohol and bring mixture nearly to boiling. Add sugar ¼ cup at a time, tasting each time. Stop when taste is right. Do not oversweeten. Serve from chafing dish or heated tureen into punch cups, with almond and 4 to 6 raisins.
Yield: 80 4-ounce servings
Mr. John Gunnarson

STAN'S EGGNOG

8 eggs
1 cup granulated sugar
1 pint brandy
1 quart rum
1 quart milk
1 quart vanilla ice cream
nutmeg

Separate egg yolks from the whites. Set aside the whites and beat the yolks vigorously. While beating, slowly add the sugar through a sifter. Slowly pour in brandy while still stir-

ring. Follow with the rum and then the milk while continuing to stir. Refrigerate 24 hours in airtight glass containers. Refrigerate the egg whites separately. When ready to serve, add the ice cream. Top with the beaten (stiff) egg whites and sprinkle with nutmeg.
Yield: 25 cups
Dr. Stanley I. Buchin

HOT CRANBERRY PUNCH
This punch has a lemonade syrup base used by my mother-in-law, Esther Howe Anderson, to concoct always different and always delightful punches with fruits and herbs from her garden.

2 cups granulated sugar
1 cup water
1 cup lemon juice
4 cups cranberry juice
4 cups pineapple juice
½ teaspoon cinnamon
½ teaspoon ginger
thin slices of oranges and lemons for garnish

Boil sugar and water over medium heat for 10 minutes. Add lemon, cranberry and pineapple juices, and spices and heat slowly until just boiling. Allow to cool slightly and pour into a warmed punch bowl. Garnish with thin orange and lemon slices.
Yield: 20 4-ounce servings
Mrs. William W. Anderson

RUM PUNCH

2 quarts Jamaican rum
1 quart brandy
1 pint peach or apricot brandy
¾ pound superfine sugar
1 quart lemon juice
2 quarts sparkling water

In a large glass, porcelain, or stainless-steel container, mix rum and brandies, cover, and let sit for 24 hours. Dissolve sugar in lemon juice. Put in punch bowl with liquor and sparkling water and large block of ice and allow to sit, stirring occasionally, for 1 hour before serving.
Yield: 50 4-ounce servings
Mrs. William W. Anderson

TOM AND JERRY HOLIDAY DRINK
This is a traditional New Year's Day recipe of my mother's, used primarily in the Midwest and the South. Can be used at other holiday parties.

16 eggs
1 bottle dark rum
1 bottle bourbon
boiling water
2 pounds confectioners' sugar (or a little more)
nutmeg

Separate eggs and beat yolks until very light and whites until stiff. Blend together, beating in confectioners' sugar to make a thick or stiff batter. For each person, spoon 1 tablespoon batter into a teacup. Add ½ ounce rum and 1 ounce bourbon. Pour boiling water to fill cup. Stir. Sprinkle on nutmeg.
Yield: 20 servings
Mrs. Helge Holst

OLD-FASHIONED RUM PUNCH
This was my grandmother's recipe.

4 quarts light rum
⅔ quart dark rum
⅔ quart Burgundy, for color
1 quart brandy
1 quart strong tea
1 quart lemon juice
⅔ quart maple syrup
⅔ pound confectioners' sugar
10 quarts soda water
lemon and orange slices

Mix everything but soda water and fruit the night before. Just before serving, add equal parts liquor and soda water, and garnish with fruit slices. Serve over large cake of ice.
Yield: 70 servings
Mrs. Everett Parker

How to Make Your Own
Olde Concord Christmas Decorations

POMANDERS
(Photo #54, page 93)

Pomanders have been used for centuries, although their use has changed in modern times. Whereas today's pomander simply conveys a scent or fragrance, the seventeenth-century housewife used hers to conteract, or cover up, the unpleasant day-to-day odors of tallow lamps, greasy hearths, and infrequent washings. Not only were pomander balls used aromatically in the seventeenth century, but they were used to an even greater extent medicinally. In times past, the herbalist and his herbs kept you well. To that end it was believed helpful to wear a small "apple of amber" (from the French *pomme d'ambre*) around your neck or waist to ward off plague, pestilence, or evil spirits. "Amber" refers to ambergris, which was the common animal fixative used in those days for scented balls.

To make a pomander, first prepare a ground-spice mixture that is one part cloves, one part nutmeg, one part allspice, one part cinnamon, and one part orris root. Orris root is the vegetable fixative we use today instead of ambergris. Mix well in an open bowl and set aside.

Select oranges that are perfect in appearance and condition. (You may prefer to use apples, lemons, limes, or quinces for your base, but oranges are traditional.) Stud the entire orange rind with whole cloves. Place the cloves close together but not so close that you run the risk of breaking the orange skin between the cloves. If you prefer variations, you can make rows or patterns of cloves. Always do the complete studding process on any one orange at one time, because the orange will become difficult to work with if it's left to stand for any length of time.

When the orange is completely studded with cloves, roll it in the spice mixture in the bowl, being sure to coat the entire surface. Place the bowl, with the fruit in it, in a warm dry place for a week or more, until the orange has dried out and hardened. Turn the orange in the spice mixture daily to ensure an even curing.

Once the drying process is completed, pomanders are traditionally tied up in ribbons so that they may be hung about the house. If you find that you have trouble with ribbons slipping off the oranges as they shrink, there are two alternatives you might want to try. The first is to leave a central cross pattern bare while studding your orange with cloves. By placing the ribbons in the "grooves," the surrounding cloves act as a barrier to hold the ribbon in place. Another solution is to simply thread ribbon through the center of the orange like a bead on a string. To do this, insert a long skewer or thick wire through the length of the orange before studding. Keep the wire in the orange while it is drying so that the hole is retained and does not shrink up. Twist the orange on the wire daily so that orange and wire do not cement themselves together. Remove the wire or skewer when the orange is dry and thread a pretty ribbon through the hole. Use a crochet hook to pull it through. Tie a big bow or knot under the base of the orange so that the ribbon cannot pull out.

These pomanders will last for many months, imparting their fragrance to rooms and houses just as they did centuries ago.

POTPOURRI

The present popularity of potpourri, scents, and fragrances is nothing new and certainly not surprising. Whether used by colonists as a necessity or by our grandmothers to perfume their bustling households, the allure has been constant down through the years. There is some deep, inner satisfaction derived from the scent of roses and other sweet smells that emanate from a potpourri on a winter's day. Who knows if it triggers pleasant thoughts of a summer day gone by, of walks taken through a well-loved garden, or if one simply enjoys the heavenly, heady fragrances of the world's best-loved flowers. Whatever the reason, a potpourri is easy to make and its enjoyment is long lasting.

Two methods of making a potpourri have been used equally over the years: one moist, the other dry. The moist method, although the more fragrant and longer lasting of the two, is not pretty to look at and is kept covered. After all, the French *potpourri* means "rotten pot," and it is from the moist version that it takes its name. The dry method is more commonly used today; it is both pretty to look at and pretty to smell.

Flowers and Leaves. A potpourri is a rather freewheeling mixture of flowers and herbs, spices, fixatives, and oils; and as such, it may be made in any combination that suits your fancy or garden. It may be sweet smelling or spicy, but, traditionally, roses and lavender are the main ingredients because they are the best at keeping their fragrance. As a rule of thumb, use the proportions of one cup petals and leaves to one teaspoon spices, one teaspoon fixative, and a drop or two of essential oils.

Whatever your choice, you undoubtedly will need a lot of rose petals. The very old varieties of rose such as the damask, the cabbage, and the French are, by far, the most fragrant and should be used if they are available to you. Pick the roses on a sunny, dry day just as they are coming into full bloom. Separate the petals from the flowers and discard any that are less than perfect. Set the petals to dry in a single layer on a drying rack that has been covered with cheesecloth, or on any similar device through which air can circulate freely. The petals should dry as quickly as possible to retain their fragrance and color. Set your drying rack in a warm, airy place (about 70° F. is ideal), being careful to avoid drafts and direct sunlight. Turn the petals occasionally for quick, even drying. They are dry when they sound like rustling leaves and snap when they are bent. Store them in an airtight jar or container, away from sunlight, until ready to make the potpourri.

Lavender, too, will be needed in quantity. Pick the lavender spikes as you did the roses—on a dry, sunny morning just as they are coming into full bloom. Hang them upside down in small bunches in your drying area until dry (a week or two). Then strip the flowers and leaves off the stems and place them in a separate airtight container. All ingredients are kept segregated until the potpourri is made.

Leaves of lemon verbena, rose-scented geraniums, and rosemary make a nice addition to the potpourri, as might a number of other fragrant herbs. If the leaves are relatively large, such as those of the lemon verbena and rose-scented geraniums, gently pick them off the stem and dry them, individually, on your rack as you did the rose petals. If the leaves are relatively small or needle-like, such as those of the rosemary, then dry them collectively by leaving them on the stem. Tie a bunch of the stems together and hang them to dry in your warm, airy place. Store as above.

Certain flowers such as bee balm, calendula petals, bachelor's buttons, and rose buds are nice to add for their visual attributes of form and color. Dry some of these in silica gel (the rose buds may be dried on the racks with the rose petals if you wish so that they will retain their shape.) Store until ready to use.

Spices. Spices of all sorts and combinations may be added, but be careful not to use those that will overpower your subtler fragrances. Cardamom and nutmeg are lovely to add to a sweet potpourri. The ground-up, dried zest of an orange or lemon peel may be added too.

Fixatives and Oils. In order to enhance and preserve the fragrances of the flower petals and leaves, you will need a fixative. One commonly used is orris root, which comes from the rhizomes of Florentine irises and has a violet aroma. Orris root is available at your druggist in either powdered or ground form. Buy the latter, for it will not detract as much from the prettiness of your potpourri.

Fragrant oils may also be bought at the drugstore, and the addition of a few drops in your mixture will strengthen the scent you wish to emphasize and will make it last longer. Use judiciously as they are potent.

Assembly. Into a big bowl put the dried ingredients: two cups of dried rose petals, one cup of dried lavender flowers and petals, and one cup combining the dried leaves of the lemon verbena, rose-scented geraniums, and rosemary. Add a handful or so of the flowers you have dried for form and color. Then add one and one-half teaspoons ground cardamom, one and one-half teaspoons ground nutmeg, one tablespoon ground orris root, and four drops oil of roses. Mix all the ingredients together gently but well and turn the entire mixture into a jar or container with a close-fitting top or stopper. Set aside in a dark, dry place for a month or six weeks, stirring occasionally so that the mixture has a chance to "work" and blend. When ready to use, put part of it, or all of it (depending on the amount you made) into a pretty bowl or container. A Chinese export bowl is a handsome and very appropriate container for potpourri, and there are special china potpourri containers with perforated lids that are very effective as well. The fragrance will last through the winter season in an open bowl,

and longer if kept in a closed or perforated container whose lid is lifted only when desired.

PINEAPPLE-LEMON CONE
(Photo #55, page 93)

Majestic fruit decorations, such as this pineapple-and-lemon-studded cone, were known to have graced the tables of the colonists in the eighteenth century. Their purpose, unlike ours today, was partly utilitarian, for it was a convenient way to display and serve an abundance and variety of fruit for dessert. And as much as it offends our aesthetic sensibilities today, these impressive creations were meant to be eaten, and they were!

Base. The base is a flat-topped wooden cone that has been painted green and that has seven rows of finishing nails studding the sides and two or three finishing nails on top. Forms such as these may be purchased (our Museum shop sells them) or, if you are particularly handy and have a home lathe, you can make one yourself. Although the wooden cones are expensive, they are preferable to the styrofoam varieties because they are much sturdier under the heavy weight of the fruit, and are reusable year after year.

Assembly. Place your wooden base on a flat plate or tray. Impale one to two dozen lemons on the nails. The number will depend on the size of your cone. You want to be firm in pushing on the fruit as it has a knack of wanting to slide off. You also want to avoid having to puncture the lemons more than once as they will not last as long if you do. In any case, some of the lemons will have to be replaced within a week's time. If "parade-dress" appeals to you, you may march your fruit right down the rows of nails. However, it is often more attractive and graceful to hammer a few extra nails in your cone and develop a more naturalistic pattern to your lemon placement.

Once your cone is bedecked with lemons, stand the loveliest pineapple you can find on the flat top of the cone, impaling it on the nails. These traditional symbols of hospitality are a most fitting choice for the tops of these handsome pyramids of fruit. However, one of the hardest aspects of making this cone is finding a level and balanced pineapple with a symmetrical yet unblemished crown. It may take a number of trips to the supermarket before you find your perfect pineapple, but the results will be worth the effort.

With all the fruit in place, tuck boxwood into all the interstices, both to cover the cone and to give the arrangement body. For a less formal effect, yew, native to New England, can be used instead of boxwood.

Adding a wonderful contrast in texture to the cross-hatching of the pineapple and the porelike skin of the lemons are the smooth white petals of the Christmas roses. These rare flowers should be dried in silica gel and gently poked into the boxwood for a very festive touch. Finally, slide glycerined laurel leaves or, for a softer effect, arborvitae, under and about the plate and base.

CRYSTALLIZED ROSE PETALS

Perhaps no other flower has been quite as loved or as written about as the rose. The eglantine rose (commonly known as the sweetbrier rose) was mentioned by William Shakespeare in a number of his plays, and it is the same rose that has been found in Concord since earliest times and still grows abundantly in Concord gardens today.

One of the prettiest ways the colonial housewife had to preserve the charm, beauty, and aroma of this perennial favorite was to candy, or crystallize, its petals. This she did often and would use the sugared petals in special, edible decorations atop desserts or cakes; or she might use them simply as an engaging confection with which to tempt a guest or special friend.

To make them, gather wild roses at the height of their perfection and wash them with a mist of cool water. Pat dry, gingerly, with paper towels. Break the roses apart very carefully and dip the individual petals in beaten egg whites and gently coat them with superfine sugar. (Tweezers and a small, soft paintbrush can be helpful tools in this step.) Place the rose petals on a cookie sheet, making sure they do not touch one another. Put the cookie sheet in full sun, or in a 250° oven until the petals are

completely dry. Store the crystallized rose petals in an airtight tin, first putting in a piece of waxed paper, then a layer of rose petals. Continue on in this fashion of paper and rose layers until all the rose petals have been stored, ending with waxed paper. Seal the tin with masking tape and keep it in a cool, dry place until ready to use. Fresh violets or mint leaves (spearmint, peppermint, or applemint) may be treated in the same fashion.

WILDFLOWER SWAG
(Photos #56 and 57, page 94)

This glorious swag of wildflowers seems to epitomize Concord's love of simplicity, sincerity, and nature. A more fitting choice to adorn the Queen Anne Room is hard to be imagined. The graceful curve of the swag sets off the balanced spaces of the unadorned 1750 paneling. The colors enhance the room by picking up the orange, yellow, and beige hues of the crewel embroidery found on the wing chair. And the wildflowers themselves, however humble and unassuming, take on a whole new festive and jewellike beauty when twined together and seen in the winter season.

Base. For ease in handling, the base is made in three parts—a curving central section and two side drops, one for each side. Cut a swag, slightly smaller than the size and shape you want, out of hardware cloth. Have your hardware store cut three angle irons to fit the back of each piece like a spine. Drill a number of holes through the angle irons and attach them securely, with wire, to the pieces of hardware cloth. This procedure will give the swag stability and prevent any flexing, which would prove so detrimental to the fragile flowers.

In order to hang the swag, affix a wire loop to the top-back of each of the side panels, and a loop to each end of the central section of the swag. You will enjoy much more success if you do this step now rather than when the swag is completed. (The handling of the finished swag should be kept to an absolute minimum.)

Spray the entire structure to match the color of the wall, mantel, or background that is to be decorated. We sprayed our base brown to camouflage the mesh and to blend in with the woodwork.

Flowers. A labor of love goes into the making of this swag as a wealth of wildflowers is collected and dried all summer long. The varieties are many and may be found along roadsides and in woods, meadows, and gardens: goldenrod, yarrow, the button-like tansy, Queen Anne's lace, yellow and orange strawflowers, ferns of assorted shapes and sizes, white and yellow statice, joe-pye weed, pearly everlasting, honesty, artemisia, wild roses, yellow day lilies, black-eyed Susans, and the always handsome tiger lilies.

Pay strict attention to the proper time for harvesting each variety of flower and, also, to their condition. Both aspects can severly affect the outcome of your flower drying. Choose flowers of good color and quality. (You will find that imperfections are magnified, somehow, in the drying process.) Cut the flowers when they are free from moisture. Flowers wet with the morning dew or from a passing shower will not dry nearly so successfully and will take a great deal longer.

Follow the rules of conservation when dealing with wildflowers. Pick only what you are going to use and no more. Cut off only the flowers and leave the plant to bloom again. And, by all means, know what wildflowers are on the protected list in your state and don't pick them!

The goldenrod (lots of it), yarrow, tansy, strawflowers, statice, joe-pye weed, pearly everlasting, honesty, and artemisia (lots of it, also), are all air-dried. Simply pick the flowers, strip off all the leaves, and tie four or five stems together in a bunch. Hang them upside-down to dry in a dark, dry place that has good air circulation. The amount of time needed for drying will vary with different varieties, but, in general, two or three weeks will be sufficient to dry most of them.

The more fragile flowers—the Queen Anne's lace, black-eyed Susans, day lilies, wild roses, and tiger lilies—are all dried in silica gel, a method that is faster but somewhat more complicated than air-drying. Directions on the details of this process are available on the packages of silica gel, as well as in the many good books available on the subject.

Press ferns between the pages of a newspaper. You will want a good number of them and a variety of shapes and sizes. Bend them into curves so that they will have a more naturalistic shape. Slip the newspapers under a rug for a few weeks until the ferns are dried.

Assembly. Gather your masses of dried wildflowers around you. You will need great quantities as it takes many more dried flowers to fill a space than it does fresh ones and you want the swag to be well covered and full looking. It is also nice to have a few extra flowers in case you have need of a replacement or a touch-up once your swag is completed.

Start with the sturdiest flowers—the goldenrod and artemisia—and insert them into your base to create a blanket of color. Build up your swag with the other varieties of flowers, keeping balance, scale, design, and color in mind. Always work from the less delicate flowers on the bottom toward the more fragile flowers on the top, thereby avoiding crushing those beneath. Tuck in ferns or pieces of ferns to add contrast and to give a feeling of foliage. Save the day lilies and the tiger lilies and put them in the swag after it has been hung as they are so easily injured and will be your focal points.

Once your swag is abundantly filled, hang the three sections on two nails. (You will have one side drop and one end of the central section on each nail.) Gently insert the day lilies and the tiger lilies, making sure to take advantage of their striking form and color.

The addition of several butterflies, to be perched on a flower here and there, give a final enchanting touch to your wildflower swag. Perhaps you can find a young friend to give you some, if you do not happen to have a butterfly collection of your own.

HERB WREATH
(Photo #58, page 94)

A puppet show in the Queen Anne Room calls for special decorations, ones that are out of the ordinary and have a charm all their own. Such is the case with the herb wreath that rings the punch bowl set out for the guests. The herbs—lady's mantle, artemisia annua, and feverfew—are chosen because of their special qualities of aroma, color, and shape, and all combine to make a most charming wreath.

Base. A modern crimp frame (a circle made of a single crimped piece of wire) was used as the base of this wreath. In the past it probably would have been fashioned out of a supple branch such as a willow or a vine. Make sure the frame is large enough to fit around the bowl you plan to use, allowing room to spare for the bushy herbs. Cover the entire frame with green floral tape to camouflage it.

Flowers. Air-dry a few branches of artemisia annua, an uncommon form of artemisia that is tall and vertical, like some of its relatives, and looks something like delicate, overgrown goldenrod. However, it is distinguished by a wonderful green-gold color and a delightful fragrance.

Lady's mantle is an herb that is a treasure for decorating not only because it is hard to find but also because of its wonderful characteristic of bushiness. This perennial herb has clusters of light green flowers that bloom all summer. Collect a number of these widespreading branches to air dry for your wreath.

The small, white and yellow, daisylike flowers of the feverfew plant are dried in silica gel. Place the flowers in the desiccant with a bend in their stems so that the flowers will appear to "look up" when arranged in the wreath.

Assembly. The wreath is made by a succession of flower bunches that you have formed in your hand and then taped onto the frame. Start with a single piece of artemisia, placing it between thumb and forefinger. (The artemisia will not be seen in the wreath. It is there for its fragrance.) To the piece of artemisia, add lady's mantle and feverfew carefully and gently until you cannot hold any more in your hand. Bind the bunch together with green floral tape and then attach it to the frame. Proceed in a similar fashion with like bunches of flowers, all the way around the frame. Because of the fullness of the lady's mantle, you will only need to go around the wreath once. The result is a lovely, fragrant, full wreath crowned with the charming feverfew flowers.

Carefully set the punch bowl inside the wreath and fill it with a special holiday punch. (In the Museum, we are careful to use a liner with our antique bowls because the liquid might damage or stain them.)

PINE CONE DECORATION
(Photo #59, page 94)

Today our concept of Christmas colors is one of red and green, but such has not always been the case. In fact, Christmas decorations of years gone by tended to follow a rule that has always been most effective: make the colors of the Christmas decoration bright and festive and correlate them with the colors already in the room. This was carried out with great effectiveness in the Museum's Chippendale Room where a pine-cone decoration, with its warm, chocolate tones and purple ribbon festoons, was a wonderful color complement to the puce hues found in the fireplace tiles, the curtains, and some of the upholstery.

Base. The backing for this decoration is made of hardware cloth—a heavy, wire mesh obtainable at any hardware store. Draw a pattern for your decoration on brown paper. (Ours had one long, straight central section with short drops on each end.) Then, using this pattern, cut out the hardware cloth base with wire cutters.

Wire a long angle iron onto the top-back of the shaped base. This will give the decoration stability and will act as a support when hanging. Wire two loops and attach them to the corners for hangers. Spraypaint the entire base brown.

Cones, Fruit, and Flowers. Selectively collect a good number of white pine cones and acorns in the spring and summer months. Cut some cones in half, producing a blossom-like effect. Leave some cones whole. Wire all of them individually by twisting a piece of wire around and among the scales of the cones. Drill small holes through the acorns, thread with wire, and twist securely. Gather a number of wired acorns in your hand and wrap them together with a wire. They are more effective used in a mass than singly.

Air-dry strawflowers in the pink and purple family and wire them together in small bunches. Attach wires to clusters of purple grapes and black grapes as well as a few blackberries and raspberries. (We used artificial fruit.)

Assembly. Plan out the whole design of the decoration before you start wiring on the individual elements. It is a good idea to place the fruits, cones, and flowers on the mesh and move them around until you are satisfied with your arrangement. Then wire them all onto the hardware cloth tightly and securely so that nothing will slide or shift when you hang the decoration. This is a very time-consuming process, but a happy thought is that once done, this decoration will last for years and may be used again and again.

Once everything has been wired into place, spray the decoration with a clear krylon spray. (Do this outside or in a well-ventilated place.) Allow the spray to dry thoroughly and then repeat this process six or seven times until a hard lacquered surface has been developed. Sprinkle the grapes with unscented talcum powder while the spray is still wet to give them a dusty look.

Back the decoration by sewing on a corresponding piece of brown felt to protect the woodwork from being scratched by the cones, the wires, or the mesh. Finish by winding purple ribbon around the decoration in a spiraling effect, tacking it in place with small unseen stitches. Complete the decoration by wiring on a handsome bow of purple ribbon in the center.

BOXWOOD TOPIARY TREE
(Photo #60, page 95)

This topiary tree, decorated with tiny presents and puce-colored bows, would have been an appropriate Christmas decoration in the mid-eighteenth century, as fanciful and geometric topiaries were well known in England and, consequently, would have been copied in the colonies. The Christmas tree as we know it, of course, was not introduced into this country until a century later in the Victorian era.

Tree Trunk. The tree trunk we used was a wooden dowel about two feet long, although a maple sapling would have been a more likely candidate in the eighteenth century. Drill three small holes in the dowel, one three inches, one ten inches, and one seventeen inches from the top. Paint the dowel dark green. Anchor the dowel in a straight-sided flower pot by surrounding it with small stones and then filling it with plaster of paris. (A ballast of sand would have been used, most likely, in earlier times.) Allow the plaster to dry completely—twenty-four hours. Wrap the pot neatly with a pretty material to celebrate the holiday season, or to match the colors of your room. Tie a festive ribbon around it.

Tree Branches. Make three arms or branches by wrapping pieces of chicken wire around rolls of wet oasis. Make the three arms about two inches in diameter, and twelve, five, and two inches in length respectively. Just as in a real tree, our topiary branches are widest at the bottom and taper up to the narrowest at the top.

Packages or Presents. Make tiny presents out of the leftover pieces of dry oasis. Use a variety of shapes and sizes, always keeping scale in mind. Wrap the oasis "presents" in tissue paper or wrapping paper. We used puce (purple) for our tree as it is the predominant color in the Museum's Chippendale Room, where the tree was placed. Tie the packages with fine colored string or worsted. Then twist the string, from the bottom or side of each package, around the head of a straight pin. That will enable you to attach the packages to the tree later on.

Ribbon Bows. Using narrow ribbon that matches the color of the ribbon tied around the pot, make a number of small bows. Put a straight pin through the back of each bow, hiding the pin.

Assembly. Starting with the longest branch, push it down onto the dowel stopping just above the bottom hole. Be sure to center the branch so that you have equal arms on both sides. Using wire, secure the bottom of the arm tightly to the bottom hole of the dowel. Repeat the process for the middle-length arm above the middle hole, and the shortest arm above the top hole. Cover all three branches completely by sticking sprigs of boxwood into the wet oasis.

Complete by attaching packages and bows all over the tree branches, where desired.

To keep the greens fresh, dribble small quantities of water along the top of the branches each day with an eye dropper, making sure not to spill on the presents or bows.

FROSTED FRUIT TREE
(Photo #61, page 95)

Guests at a Victorian wedding party, entering the hallway of the house, are greeted with this sparkling pyramid of fruit, its beauty reflected in the gilt mirror behind it.

Apples. Buy firm and unblemished red lady apples and yellow apples. You will need seven of each color. Holding each apple by its stem, coat it evenly with slightly beaten egg white. Roll the apples in a bowl partially filled with granulated sugar and make sure they are covered. Dry overnight on a cookie sheet lined with waxed paper.

Grapes. Again, buy perfect fruit if you are using fresh fruit. You will need about two pounds each of red, green, and purple grapes. Quality plastic grapes may be substituted or used in combination with the real ones as it is quite impossible to tell the difference, once frosted. However, the plastic ones do not drape as satisfactorily. Either way, keep some clusters whole and snip some into smaller bunches. Coat with egg white and spoon sugar over them, shaking gently. These do not need to be covered completely. Dry as above.

Ferns. Pick six or eight pretty ferns in late summer and place them between the pages of a newspaper. Do not allow them to touch one another. Put them under a traffic-free rug and forget them until ready to use. By that time they will be well dried and pressed. Proceed to frost them as you did the grapes.

Assembly. One might suppose that this tree has a conical base of some sort, but it does not. The form would make the fruit protrude out too far and the graceful shape of the tree would be lost. Instead, the tree is formed simply by piling the fruit upon itself. Starting with the larger yellow apples, place one in the center of a flat-topped cake plate. Take six double pointed wooded skewers about two inches long and insert them into the middle side of the central apple. Popsicle sticks that have had their ends whittled to a point can also be used. Metal skewers, however, hasten the fruit's deterioration. Place them so they are equidistant from one another and resemble spokes. Insert each of the remaining yellow apples on a spoke, butting them up to the central apple. You now have formed a wheel-like base.

Insert one skewer, about four and one-half inches long, into the center and top of the middle apple. Insert it about three inches. Push a frosted red apple down onto it, being sure to center the apple. Now you are ready to construct a second ring in exactly the same fashion as the first but, this time, using the smaller lady apples. For support, be sure the new layer of apples rests on top of those beneath. Tuck small bunches of frosted grapes in between the apples, securing them with hidden toothpicks.

Layer clusters of grapes on top of the apples, tapering the scale as you go upward. Vary the colors of the red, green, and purple grapes and secure them with toothpicks. The tree will be fourteen or fifteen inches high and, because it is frosted, will last about two weeks if it is kept in a cool, dry place.

Set the whole cake plate on a circle of frosted ferns, and for a very festive touch, top your tree with a large piece of sparkling rock candy.

KISSING-BALL
(Photo #62, page 95)

One does not know if it is the innate attractiveness and good looks of a kissing-ball or the possibility of a stolen kiss that have made this kind of decoration so popular. But whatever the reason, it is simple to make and may be made in a number of different ways.

In our 1973 exhibit, the Museum's Yellow Bedroom was depicted as if it had belonged to a young girl. Her embroidery materials were strewn on the bed and she had just finished setting up a tea party for her dolls, complete with Christmas tree and a tablecloth which she had made from ribbons. Perhaps all these things inspired her to choose the materials she did for her kissing-ball, which she hung near the window.

Take three small embroidery hoops, wrap them with pretty ribbon, and insert them one inside the other. Adjust them until the resulting six sections are of equal size. Most hoops

Nanlee Smith

54. Decoration by Mrs. Robert M. Armstrong and Mrs. Jacque R. Smith.

Bruce K. Nelson

55. Decoration by Mrs. Bruce K. Nelson and Mrs. John W. Teele.

54. *Top.* Here in the Seventeenth-Century Room are the makings for pomander balls, which were worn or placed in a room to counteract odors. The baby sleeps in a cradle nearby.

55. *Bottom.* The use of pyramids of fruits and flowers for special occasions goes far back in history all over the globe. Here, in the Green Room, dried Christmas roses were tucked into greens surrounding lemons. A pineapple surmounted the whole, for pineapples have long been symbolic of hospitality.

56. Decoration by Mrs. S. Willard Bridges, Jr. and Mrs. William F.A. Stride.

57. Decoration by Mrs. S. Willard Bridges, Jr. and Mrs. William F.A. Stride.

58. Decoration by Mrs. Richard Ferraro.

59. Decoration by Mrs. S. Willard Bridges, Jr., and Mrs. Peter A. Brooke.

56. *Top left.* Inspiration for each of the garlands used above the fireplace in the Queen Anne Room came from decorative motifs in the rococo style. In this period, many art forms seem to express femininity and were interpreted by pastel colors, undulating curves, and slender proportions. Besides the room's own special flower, Queen Anne's lace, this one includes tansy, joe-pye weed, black-eyed Susans, wild roses, goldenrod, day lilies, honesty, and even butterflies.

57. *Top right.* The detail of the wildflower swag in the Queen Anne Room shows the central design of lilies surrounded by a few of the different kinds of dried flowers.

58. *Bottom left.* The blue China-trade punch bowl in the Queen Anne Room is wreathed with dried flowers—lady's mantle and feverfew—and pale green ribbon. For this holiday party, the ladies will be served tea with an assortment of sweets and crystallized rose petals as a special treat. The gentlemen will be served negus, a spirited drink combining port, water, sugar, lemon, and nutmeg.

59. *Bottom right.* This detail of the pine cone decoration above the fireplace tiles in the Chippendale Room shows the use of air-dried straw flowers, white pine cones cut in half, and clusters of fruit (the Museum used artificial purple and black grapes, blackberries, and raspberries.)

Nanlee Smith

60. *Decoration by Mrs. W. Ward Willett.*

Nanlee Smith

Nanlee Smith

61. *Decoration by Mrs. Harvey Wheeler.*

62. *Decoration by Mrs. Austin F. Lyne and Mrs. Charles A. Morss, Jr.*

60. *Top left.* In eighteenth-century formal gardens, a feature newly introduced was the topiary tree. Although the Christmas tree as we know it had not yet made its appearance, a topiary tree like this one in the Chippendale Room might well have been a decoration for a festive occasion. This decoration also picks up the puce color in the woodwork and wallpaper behind it.

61. *Bottom left.* For our sentimental interpretation of a Victorian wedding with the front hall as its setting, a pyramid of frosted fruits graces the sideboard. The fussy lacy effect so dear to the hearts of Victorians was accomplished by placing pressed ferns, frosted with sugar, at the base. The mirror above reflects the glitter of sugar used to enhance the fruits.

62. *Above right.* A kissing ball made for the holiday hangs from ribbons in the window of the Yellow Room. Later it will be taken downstairs to hang in the front hall, where it will be "kiss as catch can" all through the holidays.

63. Decoration by Mrs. Joseph D. Fleming, Jr.
and Mrs. Elmer M. Purcell.

65. Decoration by Mrs. Paul R. Dinsmore and Mrs. S. Kenneth Neill.

64. Decoration by Mrs. Frank W. Wilson.

63. *Top left.* Here in the Reeded Room a tussy-mussy, a small bouquet whose every flower conveys a sentimental message, has just unexpectedly arrived for the young lady dressing for a Christmas ball.

64. *Bottom.* The decoration trimming the doorway in the Alcove is formed of grapes, pomegranates, and scarlet oak leaves on a background of arborvitae. A single roping of arborvitae surmounts the decoration.

65. *Top right.* Roses are frequently used in the decoration of our exhibits in the Federal Parlor; roses were very popular during this period. Rose leaves form the backing for this delicate Queen Anne's lace wreath, which is scattered with roses and repeats the relief carving under the mantle.

will fit very snugly and will need no further reinforcement, but if you feel your kissing-ball might get knocked accidently, then you may want to wire the top and the bottom (where the hoops join) to keep the hoops in place.

Tuck sprigs of boxwood up the sides of the hoops by sticking their stems under the wrappings of ribbon. Wire mistletoe onto the bottom of the hoops and then a ribbon-bow, allowing the streamers some length for a graceful flow. Tie whatever length of ribbon you desire to the top of the hoops so that you can hang it up.

This version of the kissing-ball, although extremely attractive, will not last very long as it has no way for the greens to retain, or absorb moisture. (In 1973 our exhibit ran only a very few days so it was no problem.) If you wish it to last longer you will have to replace the sprigs of boxwood or use another method such as the one used in the Museum's staircase window in the 1976 exhibit. This kissing-ball was solid in form as opposed to the openness of the one made with embroidery hoops. It used a potato for a base. Your biggest problem is to find a truly round potato of the size you want. The size of the finished ball, after all, will depend on the size of the potato you choose and on the length of the boxwood sprigs you cut so be sure to keep both things in mind.

First take two lengths of wire and wrap your potato with them as you would wrap string around a package. Twist the ends together securely at what will be the top of your kissing-ball and form them into a loop or hook.

Cut boxwood sprigs of a uniform length and insert them evenly all over the potato until it is filled in and bushy. You will find the job much easier if you cut the boxwood on a slant, thereby making sharp, pointed ends.

Once your kissing-ball is well covered, wire some mistletoe and insert it into the bottom of the ball and then, in the same place, attach a cascading bow of ribbons. Narrow red ribbon or white velvet ribbon have both been used with great effectiveness. Cut a length of matching ribbon and thread it through your wire loop on the top of your ball. Then hang it in a place that will be the most favorable for catching that special someone for a kiss.

This kissing-ball will last for several weeks due to the moisture found within the potato itself. You can help it along, by keeping it in a cool place and giving it a daily misting of water.

Other solid kissing-balls may be made in the same manner but by using a base of wet oasis or spagnum moss wrapped in chicken wire or hardware cloth instead of a potato. A styrofoam ball may also be used but be aware that it has the same problem as that of the embroidery hoops—no method by which you may keep the greens fresh. Moreover, if you try to replace the greens, the styrofoam may have a tendency to crumble.

But whatever method you use, a kissing-ball is bound to bring you a great deal of pleasure, in more ways than one!

TUSSY-MUSSY
(Photo #63, page 96)

No one is quite sure where the fascinating name tussy-mussy came from or how it came to be. No one even agrees on how to spell it: one finds tussie-mussie, tussey-mussey, or tussy-mussie, and there are undoubtably still more variations. However, the flowers that were chosen to be included in these charming bouquets of the eighteenth and nineteenth centuries were very specific indeed, for they conveyed a special message in a floral vocabulary that was well understood by everyone in those days.

The young lady of our Christmas exhibit, dressing for a Christmas ball, has just been surprised and delighted by the delivery of a tussy-mussy. The flowers and herbs that have been so carefully and thoughtfully included are roses for true love, marjoram for joy, southernwood for constancy, luneria (also called honesty) for honesty, violets for fidelity, and ferns for fascination. What young lady would not have been left breathless on receiving such an ardent nosegay?

The language of flowers is endless and it is the rare flower that does not have a meaning. (And some of the meanings are not nice!) One is limited only by one's own imagination, or by the occasion, in order to make an appropriate tussy-mussy for a loved one or a special friend. They may be made of either dried or fresh flowers and herbs but because our Olde Concord Christmas exhibit ran for over a week, a dried bouquet was the obvious choice for us.

Flowers and Herbs. Dry small red roses or rose buds and violets in silica gel. Air-dry the marjoram, southernwood, and luneria by hanging it in small bunches in a warm, dry, airy place. Press a few small ferns. You will want your flowers or sprigs of herbs to be about six or eight inches in length.

Tussy-Mussy Holder. Cut a circle of stiff paper about four inches in diameter. Make a small hole directly in the center of the circle through which the stems will pass. Make several cuts from the outside edge toward the center of the circle; overlap each cut about one-half inch over the next section. Glue together to form the circle of paper into a shallow cone. Lay a pretty paper doily or a circle of real lace on the cone. It should extend about one-half inch beyond the edge of the cone. Carefully glue it, or stitch it, onto the stiff paper foundation.

Assembly. Starting with the roses in the center, gather your dried flowers and herbs into a bunch in your hand. Fashion a simple yet pleasing arrangement or, if you wish, make concentric circles of the different flowers. In order to complement the colors in the Museum's Reeded Room, we took the liberty of adding touches of tansy to our bouquet as we needed a stronger yellow color than the more appropriate jonquil (I desire a return of affection) or ranunculus (you are radiant with charms) would impart.

Wire the nosegay of flowers and herbs together about three inches from the bottom. Cover the stems with florist tape, if desired, although this would obviously not have been done in the past.

Insert your tussy-mussy into the small center hole in the lacy holder and tie a narrow velvet ribbon around the stems, forming a pretty bow with long streamers.

POMEGRANATES, GREEN GRAPES, AND SCARLET OAK LEAVES
(Photo #64, page 96)

This decoration topped the doorway between the Alcove and the Federal Parlor and was constructed of green grapes, pomegranates, and scarlet oak leaves set against a background of arborvitae.

Base. Cut a rectangular piece of heavy cardboard (carton variety) for your base. Its size will depend upon the proportions of your doorway and room. Wrap the cardboard in chicken wire, making it just as secure and flat as you can. Be sure there are no sharp protruding ends. Make two sturdy hooks out of wire and attach them near the top of the back. Weave arborvitae into the chicken wire, being aware that there is a front and a back side to this flat evergreen. Cover all the chicken wire completely and the edges as well.

Pomegranates. In the New England area pomegranates come into the grocery stores in early October, and they must be bought then if they are to be dried by Christmastide. We picked warm rusty hues to match a particular color in the Museum's Alcove, but you will find that there is quite a wonderful array of reds, pinkish reds, and orangish reds from which to choose. Buy only perfect and unblemished fruit. Cut a few pomegranates in half as some will be shown open and, consequently, must be dried that way. Place the whole and cut fruit in a cool, dry place for a good two months, turning them now and then so that they will dry evenly. When thoroughly dry, thread sturdy wire through each fruit. Sometimes it is necessary to hammer a small nail through the tough skin to make the threading easier.

Grapes. As our exhibit lasted ten days there was no possibility of using fresh green grapes, so we frosted some plastic ones. To do that, beat an egg white and brush it onto the grapes. Roll the grapes in sugar until well coated and then set on a rack to dry. Attach a wire near the top and the bottom of each cluster of grapes. Not only are the grapes heavy and two points of attachment better than one, but also you often want a graceful curve in your cluster, and two wires will enable you to achieve the effect you want whereas one will not.

Leaves. Leaves from scarlet oak trees are gathered at the height of their color and while they are still supple. Only pick leaves that are whole and blemish-free. Wipe them clean. (In Revolutionary times, leaves would have been simply pressed between the pages of a book, but because our leaves were gathered a good six weeks before they were to be used, and we wanted them to retain their vivid color and sheen, we used more modern methods.) Place a leaf between two sheets of waxed paper with the waxed sides next to the leaf. Iron your leaf, using a low setting, and be ready to take the iron off immediately when the wax has melted. Carefully remove both papers from the leaf while still hot and flexible. Set the waxy leaf on a baking rack to cool and harden. Store in a covered box until ready to use.

Assembly. The construction needs to take into consideration the fact that this arrangement will be viewed well above eye level. It is a good idea to do your assembly in place and step back occasionally so as to view the arrangement in proper perspective. It can make the difference between something you are pleased with and something you are not.

The two half pomegranates, surrounded by a cluster of grapes on either side, were our focal points and we wired them to our base first. The rest of the pomegranates followed with an eye for grace and naturalness. Avoid placing everything on the same plane or angle. When you are satisfied with the arrangement of your fruit (and this step takes patience), then tuck in the scarlet oak leaves here and there. Again, strive for as natural a look as possible. Poke more arborvitae in your completed arrangement to soften any harsh lines or to cover any mechanics that show.

As the ten days of the exhibit progressed, a sprig or two of arborvitae was added to take up the slack as the greens became dryer and less dense.

WREATH OF QUEEN ANNE'S LACE
AND ROSES
(Photo #65, page 96)

Base. Cut a thick piece of cardboard to correspond with the size wreath you wish to make. Cover the cardboard with pieces of oasis shaped to fit the circle's configuration. (Oasis was chosen for convenience sake and because lightness was desired due to the fragility of the flowers. In 1810, however, the most likely choice would have been moss.) Secure the oasis to the cardboard form by wrapping with strips of cheesecloth. Wind tailor's thread around the wreath in the same fashion to tie it down further. Attach a hook made of wire to the back of the wreath.

Cover the front of the wreath with pale-colored, air-dried hydrangea, poking the stems through the cheesecloth and into the oasis. This is simply a filler and will not be seen in the finished wreath. Encircle the wreath's edge with glycerined rose leaves by tucking them under the tailor's thread on the back.

Flowers. The airy grace and delicacy of the Federal period is echoed here by the choice of flowers. Queen Anne's lace (wild carrot) was picked in the summer when the florets were just in full bloom. A great many of these lacy flowers (small size) were dried, upside down, in covered tins filled with silica gel. Enough of a stem was left on each flower to enable it to be inserted into the oasis when dried. Little bush roses were picked at their prime, wired individually, and also were dried in silica gel. Once processed, the Queen Anne's lace and the roses were brushed free of any excess silica gel and then were stored in airtight tins to which a small amount of silica gel had been added to ensure freedom from moisture. The tins were sealed with tape and stored.

Ribbon. This unique pattern of wired velveteen ribbon was copied from the relief carving of the mantel in the Federal Parlor, the room in which this wreath hung. Pink velveteen ribbon was chosen for the front, to match a color in the room's wallpaper; white velveteen ribbon was chosen for the back. Place the white ribbon on your work table with the back side facing up. Run thin florist wire down the center of the ribbon. Dot the edges of the ribbon with household glue, place the pink ribbon on top of it (velveteen side up), and seal along the edges. Allow to dry thoroughly. (Again, in 1810, ladies might have used a vine instead of our wire and either sewn the edges of the ribbon together or used a flour paste instead of our modern glue.)

Assembly. Cover the entire base with Queen Anne's lace and then dot with the delicate roses. Bend the wired ribbon to resemble the Adam-style decoration so typical of the Federal period, as we did, to match our woodwork, and attach, by means of wire, to the back of the wreath.

BIBLIOGRAPHY FOR MAKING YOUR OWN

OLDE CONCORD CHRISTMAS DECORATIONS

BOOKS

Bacon, Richard M. *The Forgotten Art of Growing, Gardening and Cooking with Herbs.* Dublin, N.H.: Yankee Inc., 1972.

Berrall, Julia S. *A History of Flower Arrangement.* New York: Studio Publications, 1953.

Burke, L. *The Language of Flowers.* Los Angeles: Price/Stern/Sloan, 1965.

Clark, Janet, Collins, Mary Alice, and Collins, Gary. "The Naturalist." *Botanical Art.* Provo, Utah: Press Publishing, 1973.

Crockett, James Underwood, Tanner, Ogden, and the Editors of Time-Life Books. *Herbs.* Alexandria, Va.: Time-Life Books, 1977.

Doole, Louise Evans. *Herbs: How to Grow and Use Them.* New York: Sterling Publishing, 1962.

Earle, Alice Morse. *Old Time Gardens.* New York: Macmillan, 1901. Reissued by the Singing Tree Press, Detroit, Michigan, 1968.

Favretti, Rudy F., and DeWolf, Gordon P. *Colonial Gardens.* Barre, Mass.: Barre Publishers, 1972.

Floyd, Harriet. *Plant It Now, Dry It Later.* New York: McGraw-Hill, 1973.

Garland, Sarah. *The Complete Book of Herbs and Spices.* New York: Viking, 1979.

Leighton, Ann. *Early American Gardens.* Boston: Houghton Mifflin, 1970

Scobey, Joan, and Myers, Norma. *Gifts from your Garden.* Indianapolis and New York: Bobbs-Merrill, 1975.

Simmons, Adelma Grenier. *A Merry Christmas Herbal.* New York: William Morrow, 1968.

Squires, Mabel. *New Trends in Dried Arrangements and Decorations.* New York: M. Barrows; distributed by William Morrow, 1967.

Thompson, Dorothea Schnibben. *Creative Decorations with Dried Flowers.* New York: Hearthside Press, 1965.

Vance, Georgia S. *The Decorative Art of Dried Flower Arrangement.* Garden City, N.Y.: Doubleday, 1972.

PAMPHLETS AND PERIODICALS

An Aromatic Garden. Concord, Mass.: Concord Antiquarian Society, 1963.

"Herbs: Fragrant Finds." *House Beautiful,* November 1979.

Index